Chestnut Hill
The New Class

Lauren Brooke

SCHOLASTIC

With special thanks to
Elisabeth Faith

Scholastic Children's Books,
Euston House, 24 Eversholt Street,
London NW1 1DB, UK
A division of Scholastic Ltd
London ~ New York ~ Toronto ~ Sydney ~ Auckland
Mexico City ~ New Delhi ~ Hong Kong

First published in the US by Scholastic Inc., 2005
This edition published in the UK by Scholastic Ltd, 2006

10 digit ISBN: 0 439 95088 0
13 digit ISBN: 978 0439 95088 6

Printed in the UK by CPI Bookmarque, Croydon, CR0 4TD

10 9 8 7 6 5 4

The right of Lauren Brooke to be identified as the author of this work
has been asserted by her in accordance with the Copyright, Designs and
Patents Act, 1988.

Papers used by Scholastic Children's Books are made from wood grown
in sustainable forests.

For Graeme,
my rock in all things

Chapter One

"Dylan, we're almost there. Wake up, honey."

Dylan Walsh blinked her eyes open. Glancing out the window, she saw whitewashed fences lining lush green pastures. "What?" Dylan murmured. "Why'd you guys let me go to sleep?"

"We just got off the interstate a few minutes ago," her dad explained.

"You didn't miss anything." Dylan's mom looked over her shoulder into the backseat of the family SUV. "I thought you probably needed the rest."

Dylan rolled her eyes before she brushed her red hair behind her ears and turned her gaze back out the window. Dylan was relieved to know she'd soon be escaping her mother's overprotective ways. It was true that she hadn't been able to sleep a wink the night before. There had been too many things going through her head. She'd been looking forward to this day for so long – she was really on her way to Chestnut Hill! She searched the fields for any signs of horses, trying to

1

gauge how close they were to the school. She wondered if all of Virginia was this picturesque.

Dylan followed the stretch of fence toward the horizon and her heart pounded when she saw the brick pillars that marked the entrance to the esteemed boarding school.

"This is it!" she yelled, recalling the first time she had visited the school. After the prospective-student weekend that spring, Dylan had been set on coming to Chestnut Hill.

She rolled down the window to get a better glimpse of the iron gates at the start of the drive. As her dad turned the car, Dylan's eyes focused on the Chestnut Hill crest. The chestnut tree (*what else?* she thought delightedly) with spreading roots and branches was worked into the ornate iron gate, along with the profile of a horse's head.

White rail fences continued on either side of the driveway, and Dylan shielded her eyes from the sun to scan the paddocks for the Chestnut Hill horses. She thought they were all beautiful, but she held her breath as she searched for one pony in particular.

Before she could find a familiar brown-and-white coat, the car turned to follow the gravel driveway, and the rest of the grounds came into view. Dylan leaned forward as they approached Old House, the magnificent white colonial building that had been the original school over one hundred years ago. With its tall white pillars, it gave Chestnut Hill a look of great Southern tradition. Now Old House just held faculty and administration offices, and the classrooms and science labs were in classic redbrick buildings on the other side of the campus. Ever since the fourth grade, when she read about it in *Horse and Rider* magazine, Dylan had wanted to attend Chestnut Hill for its top-tier riding programme. *I can't believe I'm actually here*, she thought, with a shiver of excitement. From the moment she had laid eyes on the campus that spring, she had been imagining this moment. Everything about the school was the best money could buy: the Olympic-size swimming pool, the indoor track, the art studio complete with ceramics workshop and kiln. And the school was known for high academic standards that prepared students for acceptance into the most competitive colleges, which pleased her parents.

Mr Walsh took a left turn, following the signs to the dorms on the north side of the campus. There were six houses, where students slept, studied, and generally hung out. Dylan already knew that she was in Adams House, which, very conveniently, was the dorm closest to the stable yard. She slid across the leather seat so she could look out the other window and tapped a drum roll with her fingers as they passed the wooden stables. *I'm going to be able to walk to the barn in less than five minutes*, she thought. *I'll be the most dedicated rider at Chestnut Hill. Just wait until team tryouts!*

Inside, a girl was carrying two buckets to the end stall. As the girl opened the door, Dylan caught sight of a magnificent black horse and twisted around so she could keep looking.

"Honey, you'll get whiplash if you keep turning your neck like that!" Mrs Walsh warned in a teasing tone.

Dylan straightened up, meeting her mother's eyes in the vanity mirror on the front passenger visor. "You need to brush your hair," Mrs Walsh told her. "It's flipping up again." She reached up to smooth her own neat red bob, but her tresses were already sleek and perfectly in place. Dylan might have inherited her mom's hair colour, but she sure didn't have the same patience to style and sculpt it.

"Maybe I'll just wear my hard hat." Dylan grimaced, running her fingers through her thick hair. "Then no one will notice." Her mom had been trying to persuade her to get a fringe, but she preferred having it all the same length, even if she needed a clip or a ponytail holder to keep it from falling into her eyes. "Hey, Dad, if you stop right now, I can get my hat out of the back."

Mr Walsh raised his eyebrows. "If we stop now, you'll disappear into the barn. Then you'd need a shower before you could pass your mom's inspection."

Dylan snapped her fingers. "You got me," she grinned. *Dad is so cool*, she thought, as she watched him pat her mom on the hand. *He totally gets me*. Her mom reached back and handed her a tortoiseshell hair clip. As Dylan reached for it, she switched off the DVD player built into the back of the front seat. She didn't mind not being able to watch the end of *Charlie's Angels*. Right now, real life was about one hundred times more exciting!

Dylan shifted to the middle of the backseat so she

could look out the front window. The road ahead was almost completely jammed with sports cars, SUVs, and luxury sedans. There didn't seem to be any parking spaces close to the dorm.

"Let's just stop here," Mr Walsh said, pulling over to the curb. "We can carry your luggage to the dorm."

Dylan had her hand on the door handle before her dad had even turned off the ignition. She jumped out onto the gravel path and took a deep breath. The air held a hint of autumn, but the sun, when it wasn't behind the clouds, was still at its summer strength. Everywhere Dylan looked, girls were getting out of cars, their arms full of garment bags and backpacks. Dylan followed her father around to the back of the SUV and pulled out the smaller of her two black suitcases. Mr Walsh let out a groan as he tested the weight of the larger bag.

"Come on, Dad. Here's your chance to prove what your country club membership does for you," Dylan said with a laugh. She doubted her dad had ever even been to the club's gym. He pretty much belonged for the golf and tennis, which he always ended up playing with his business partners. Without waiting to hear his reply, Dylan headed up the sidewalk in the direction of the dorms. She paused at the bottom of the sidewalk that led to the front door and tipped her h⟍ ⟍back to take in the white four-storey building. The⟍ and parents on the steps leading up t⟍ porch. Nobody had to wear the school⟍ and everyone seemed to be taking a⟍

freedom. Like Dylan, lots of girls had on jeans and casual fitted tops, which was a relief. Dylan's mom had tried to get her to wear a pleated linen skirt with a cashmere tank, arguing that Dylan should try to make a good first impression.

The front porch cleared, and Dylan made her way up the steps and through the double doors. The foyer in Adams House seemed almost as busy as the unloading area outside and twice as noisy. Dylan caught her breath. In front of her, on either side of the room, was a formal double staircase that swept upward in a swoosh of crimson carpet. At the top of the stairs, a Chinese-style vase with a colourful and elaborate arrangement of flowers sat on a polished antique table. Sunlight streamed in through a beautiful stained-glass window on the second floor, making Dylan squint. *I feel like I'm in* Gone with the Wind, she thought. She hovered uncertainly, not having a clue where she should go.

"Excuse me!" An older student carrying a cello case stopped right in front of her.

"Oh, sorry," Dylan said, embarrassed, realizing she was blocking the door. She stepped to one side and placed her suitcase on the waxed hardwood floor. *Way to go, Walsh. No better way to look like a first-year student than standing right in the doorway with a dumb look on your face.* She took a deep breath and noticed a lovely scent of jasmine in the air. She tracked the aroma to another arrangement of flowers, this one in a cut glass vase on a polished maple table, the top of which was ▯led with light. Dylan glanced up to see a magnificent chandelier hanging above her, dripping with crystals. She couldn't believe this was campus housing. It looked more like an interior design showcase.

"Dylan Walsh?" A smiling woman with dark curly hair appeared beside her. She glanced down at a clipboard and then back at Dylan. "Welcome to Adams House. Don't worry," she said. "This is the only day of the year when all chaos breaking loose is officially allowed." She held out her hand. "I'm Mrs Herson, your housemother. If you have any problems settling in, come see me and I'll try my best to help." Mrs Herson's brown eyes twinkled as she handed Dylan a map. "Noel Cousins, our dorm prefect, will show you where your room is, if you're ready."

"That would be great," Dylan said, reaching down for her suitcase.

Mrs Herson waved to a tall girl with wavy auburn hair who was just coming down the staircase. "Noel," she called. "This is Dylan Walsh. Can you take her up to Room Two?"

"Sure," the senior nodded, walking over.

"Noel is co-captain of the senior jumping team," Mrs Herson told Dylan. "So you already have something in common."

"Co-captain? That's great!" Dylan said, standing up a little straighter as she made eye contact with the senior. "I mean, isn't that what everyone wants? If they're in the riding programme, I mean." She winced. *What was going on?* Dylan was used to being so composed and knowing just what to say, but her words sounded all jumbled.

Noel smiled at the compliment. "I'd like to say it's not a big deal, but…"

"You don't want to lie, right?" Dylan relaxed enough to grin at the senior. She looked around for her parents, and, spotting them in the middle of the foyer, she waved for them to come over.

The Walshes followed Noel up the scarlet-carpeted staircase. Halfway up, the prefect paused and pointed down at a pair of doors leading off the foyer. "Before I forget, the seventh-grade common room and study hall are through there," she told Dylan. "I'm sure you'll log plenty of hours in those rooms."

As Dylan leaned forward to look down the corridor, a girl with her hair in cornrows started down the stairs, waving to someone below. She accidentally bumped against Dylan as she tried to get past. "Hey, watch it, Tanisha," Noel warned and gave Dylan an apologetic smile. "Typical upperclassman attitude. They forget they were rookies once, too!"

"I heard that," Tanisha called over her shoulder.

Listening to their banter Dylan bit her lip. Right now, it was hard to imagine she'd ever feel that comfortable around this place. It wasn't like her to be overwhelmed. She vaguely remembered her first day of kindergarten, and even then, she'd had a very practical, can-do attitude about taking on new things.

At the top of the stairs Noel turned left and walked down a hallway to a second, narrower flight of stairs.

"Your dorm room is up here," she explained. "You know, I started off in Room Two. I've always thought it's kind of lucky. Every year that I've been here, a first-year student from Room Two has made it onto the equestrian team."

"That's good news. I'm hoping to try out for the team," Dylan admitted, her heart beating faster.

"Yeah?" Noel glanced at her. "Competition's going to be tough this year, then. I know that Lynsey Harrison, who's rooming with you, is trying out, too." She paused to wait for Dylan's parents, who were looking rather out of breath. "Everyone gets used to all of the stairs after a while! There is a rickety elevator in the back, but Mrs Herson gives us a lecture on the importance of exercise if she catches us using it."

Noel held open the heavy fire doors at the top of the stairs, then led the way down a broad hall, past open doors where Dylan caught glimpses of girls unpacking. Her stomach flipped again as Noel stopped. This was it! Her room at Chestnut Hill!

"Welcome to Adams Room Two," Noel declared, opening the door. "You're rooming with Felicity Harper and Lynsey Harrison. You have a couple of hours to unpack and have a look around and then, at five o'clock, the school will be meeting in the chapel for our first convocation of the year." Noel stepped aside to allow Dylan to enter. "If you need anything, you can head down to Room Five. We're all seniors. We're a little more sane than the underclassmen. They'll calm down, though. It's just because it's the first day."

"Oh, it's OK," Dylan said. "I can handle a little insanity now and then."

"That's good to hear." A dimple flashed in Noel's cheek as she gave Dylan's parents a courteous smile. "Later," she said with a wave before slipping from the room.

Dylan let out a sigh. She hoped she had made a good impression.

Her mother stepped past her, hanging Dylan's garment bag over a chair. "Oh, this is lovely! Your lilac bedsheets will look fabulous against those floral drapes." She went over to feel the material. "You really lucked out."

Dylan followed her mom and looked around. There were three twin beds in the room, each with a matching cedar wardrobe and dresser with a pull-out desk top. The wood was the colour of warm honey, glowing in the sunlight that poured through the window at the far end of the room. It appeared that the bed immediately underneath the window had already been taken. Four cognac-coloured leather suitcases with the initials *LAH* were stacked next to it, and the bed itself was covered with shoe boxes and garment bags. Dylan set her own suitcase just inside the door.

Dylan's dad heaved the other bag over the threshold and straightened up, rubbing his back. "And I thought *you* packed too much. I pity whoever carried *her* luggage up those stairs," he joked, nodding toward the pile of bags by the window.

"That's right, Dad!" Dylan responded. "You should

never take me for granted. See what an easygoing daughter I am?"

"Yes, an easygoing daughter who begged incessantly for three years to go away to boarding school," her dad replied in a slightly accusatory tone.

Dylan knew that her father had wanted her to stay at home. She was an only child, and her dad had always treated her as though she were a friend as much as a daughter. They would swap jokes at dinner, go fishing on weekends, and, once in a while, go trail riding together. Dylan thought it was ironic – her dad had given her his love of horses, and that love had made her want to attend a boarding school over four hundred miles from home.

She walked to the far end of the room and leaned her elbows on the windowsill. The view looked straight across campus, but more importantly, it had a great view of the stable yard, where she could see a beautiful bay gelding being led in from the field.

"Look at the lines on that Thoroughbred. I bet he can really jump, huh?" Dylan's dad said as he joined her at the window. "I guess we would take him at Riverlea."

Dylan and her dad liked to daydream that they would buy a ranch out West and name it Riverlea. They'd have a dozen ponies and horses and then some cattle. Dylan knew it would never happen – for starters, she was more focused on equitation and jumping than riding Western and driving cattle – but it was fun to talk about. They sometimes did it just to tease Dylan's mom, who would consider moving to a ranch only if she could fly her hair stylist out weekly and get Prada home-delivered.

Mr Walsh pointed to a snazzy chestnut backing out of a trailer.

Dylan felt her stomach flip with excitement as she watched the everyday commotion of the stable: buckets, haynets, lead ropes, travelling wraps, horses, horses, horses! *Get me down there!* She couldn't wait to start pitching in. She'd spent most of the summer hanging out with her friends at the local stables, riding every day. Her instructor had let her try different mounts all summer, so it had felt as if she had half a dozen gorgeous ponies of her own. But the last few days had been filled with packing and sorting out her bedroom at home, so Dylan was anxious to get into the saddle again.

"Look at this set!" Mrs Walsh exclaimed, eyeing the suitcases on Dylan's roommate's bed and running her fingers over the largest one. "I'm sure I saw one just like it in Takashimaya on Fifth Avenue."

"They must belong to Lynsey Harrison," Dylan told her.

Mrs Walsh straightened up, beaming. "The Harrisons! Of course! I knew I'd heard the name. There was an article in *Vanity Fair* last month that mentioned Mrs Harrison's last fundraising event. The banquet was held at their home, and it was such a beautiful house. I'm sure Lynsey will make a wonderful friend for you, Dylan."

"Mom! Like I'd choose her as a friend because her

family has enough money to be featured in *Vanity Fair*!" Dylan said. *Why does mom always get so hung up on America's A-List?* She frowned.

Her dad held up his hands in a peacemaking gesture. "Whoa, I'm sure that's not what your mom meant. After all, any of the girls here are going to come from…" He looked left then right and dropped his voice to a whisper, "…moneyed backgrounds."

Dylan grinned and threw a pillow at him from the selection on the bed closest to her.

"Is that the bed you want, honey?" Mrs Walsh asked. "We'll help you unpack."

"Um, it's OK, Mom. I think I can handle it. Anyway, I thought I'd wait until Felicity arrives so we can see who wants which bed." *In other words, I'm ready for you to leave so I can go check out the horses*, she translated silently, catching her father's eye.

"Come on, hon. I'm sure Dylan can handle it. If we linger too long, she might actually think about how much she'll miss us. We don't want her to do that."

"Dad!" Dylan didn't want them to think she didn't want them around at all, but her urge to explore was too strong to suppress.

He caught her up in a huge hug, planting a kiss on the top of her head. "You have your cell phone, so be sure to call us if you need anything," he told her. "And even if you don't."

"Sure thing," Dylan replied, her voice muffled as she pressed her head into her father's shoulder.

She hugged her mom next and, as Dylan inhaled the

familiar Amouage perfume, a wave of homesickness gripped her. *This is going to be tougher than I thought*. It was going to be so weird being away from home for this long; this was way different from summer camp, where it was for just a few weeks, or from visiting her grandparents' house in the country. "Call us later," Mrs Walsh told her, reaching out to tuck a strand of hair behind Dylan's ear. "And don't forget your Aunt Ali is here for you."

"Yeah, right. Me and two hundred other girls," Dylan pointed out, but she smiled to show she was joking. Dylan hadn't known what to think when she had first heard that her aunt had taken over as Director of Riding at Chestnut Hill. Dylan's parents had already signed all her admittance paperwork, so it had been too late for her to change her mind. Dylan had always loved visiting Ali's stables in Kentucky, but this was different. She couldn't help but think that it would be awkward living on the same campus and having Ali as her riding instructor. *So much for my new independence!* Plus, Dylan didn't want the other girls thinking that she was going to get any favoritism from Ali. She wanted to make it at Chestnut Hill on her own. But right now, Dylan had to admit that the thought of a familiar face was sort of comforting. *Great. I'll be wanting a pacifier next.*

"I'll call later," she promised her parents. "Or you can call me when you get home." She walked to the door and watched them all the way down to the end of the hall. They turned and waved before disappearing through the double doors, and Dylan went back into the room. Suddenly it felt very empty. She sat down on the edge of the bed as a funny sensation, kind of like the butterflies she felt before a riding competition, hit her stomach. *Get a grip*, she told herself. *I'm at the best school in Virginia, which has an incredible riding programme, and my favorite pony in the whole world is waiting for me down in the stable.* She lay back on the bed and closed her eyes. She had a framed photo of Morello, the paint gelding, in her backpack, but she could picture him just as clearly in her head.

She'd first met him that summer when she'd spent a couple of weeks on her aunt's farm in Kentucky. Dylan smiled as she thought back to how quickly she'd become smitten with the pony. He had the cutest personality ever! He was adventurous and mischievous – Ali had said that Dylan and Morello had a lot in common. The first time Dylan had seen him, Morello had been loose in the stables, snuffling at the feed room door. Ali had quickly caught him and put him back in his stall, playfully reprimanding the pony as she slid home the bottom bolt. Morello could undo the top lock with his teeth, Ali explained. Then she told the story about the time he wandered up to the farmhouse and was caught pushing his way through the kitchen screen door.

Morello could be a challenge in the stable, but he was a dream in the ring. He had a great rhythmic pace, and his jumps exploded with energy. Dylan had never known a pony that made riding such fun.

And, while Dylan didn't want to flatter herself, she thought Morello had been just as taken with her. By the end of her stay, he would whinny whenever he saw her and come to her at the paddock gate.

Dylan's apprehension about Ali being accepted as the riding director quickly dissolved when she heard that Morello would make the move, too. Of course! He would be perfect for Chestnut Hill. And so would Ali. Her mom had made a big point about how this job was a great opportunity for Ali – a fresh start. Dylan knew her aunt was a talented instructor. Her students had dominated at the show they went to when Dylan was visiting.

Dylan thought about the photo of Morello in her bag. It had been taken at the Lexington Horse Show, where they had placed third in the Turnout class. Dylan had wanted to compete in a jumping class, but her mom insisted Ali would be busy enough with her regular students. Still, when Dylan claimed the yellow rosette, Mrs Walsh had acted like she'd won a ribbon at a major competition – and on reflection, Dylan thought she'd done pretty well to get Morello's white patches as clean as she had, and her braids were always neat and tight. Not all judges would rank a paint that high against all the stylish ponies at an A-level show.

Dylan looked up at the sound of the door opening. She felt her heart jolt as she prepared herself for the fact that her parents had probably come back for more good-byes. Instead, it was Noel Cousins who smiled in at her before stepping back to let a petite girl with shoulder-length blond hair enter the room.

Dylan stood up and helped the girl drag in her suitcases. "Welcome to Room Two!" she said, feeling like a veteran. Acting confident seemed to ease the butterfly battle in her stomach.

"Thanks." The girl smiled, pulling her hair back from her cute, heart-shaped face.

"Dylan, this is Felicity," Noel said. "I thought you could show her around. Just make sure you're both at the convocation."

"No problem." Dylan waited for Noel to shut the door behind her before turning to her new roommate. "How are you doing, Felicity?"

"I haven't been called that in ages," the girl replied, almost in a whisper. "It sounds so formal. You can just call me Honey."

Dylan blinked when she heard her new roommate's polished accent, but she didn't miss a beat. "Nice to meet you, Honey. I'm Dylan. I'm from Connecticut."

"Oh, I'm from … well, I used to live in London, in England. We've only just moved out here – my father is a professor at the University of Virginia," Honey explained. She nodded toward the suitcases on the far bed. "Are they yours?"

"No!" Dylan said quickly. "They belong to Lynsey Harrison. I like to think of her as BBB."

Honey turned and raised a thin blond eyebrow.

"Best Bed Bagger," Dylan translated, her face

perfectly straight. "I mean, I guess it's first come, first served, so I don't really blame her."

Honey smiled. "So we get to choose between the other two, then?"

"You go first, I'm cool with either one."

"Well, if you're sure you don't mind, I'll take this one." Honey pointed to the bed nearest the door. She skirted Dylan's bed and lifted up a stylish plaid backpack. She unzipped the front pocket and pulled out a stack of photographs.

"Hey, he's gorgeous!" Dylan exclaimed, spotting a picture of a showy chestnut pony jumping over parallel bars. "Is he yours?"

"He was," Honey confirmed with a wistful sigh. "His name's Rocky. My parents bought him for me when I was nine, but I had to leave him in England." Honey reached out to trace her finger across the glass in the photo frame.

"That must have been really hard," Dylan said sympathetically. She had never had a pony of her own, but she knew how difficult it had been saying goodbye to Morello after riding him for only two weeks.

She figured it would be kind of rude to head straight for the stable yard now that Honey had arrived. She started to unpack, almost wishing she had taken her parents' offer to help as she realized just how much she had brought with her – her school uniform, riding stuff, clothes for wearing around the dorm, clothes for formal dinners, not to mention books and photos. And at the bottom of the case, there was a stuffed panda bear named Pudding that her grandmother had knitted when Dylan was a baby. He was a bit squashed after being stuffed in the oversized suitcase, but she gave him a shake, pummeled his nose back into shape, and propped him on her pillow.

Honey glanced over and caught her eye. For a moment Dylan paused. *Is it totally babyish bringing a stuffed bear to boarding school?* But then Honey wordlessly took out a small brown bear and tucked him under the top of her duvet, before flashing a grin at Dylan.

"There was no way I was coming here without Woozle!" she joked.

Relaxing, Dylan unwrapped the layer of tissue paper from around the first photograph. It showed her dad holding up a sign for his engineering company's new branch, with his other arm around Dylan's mom. The next photo was one of Dylan standing next to Morello, the yellow ribbon clipped to his bridle.

"Oh, do you ride, too?" Honey asked, leaning over to look. "What a fabulous pony!"

"This is Morello. He's actually here at Chestnut Hill. He's a little spoiled. He'll probably expect a bunch of organic carrots off a silver platter when he sees me," Dylan told her. "I was about to go down to the stable before you got here. Do you want to head down together?" She glanced at her watch. "We've got lots of time before convocation."

Honey's brown eyes lit up. "That sounds good."

Dylan grinned, figuring things couldn't get much better – and she'd only been at Chestnut Hill for an hour. She sprang to her feet. "Let's go!"

Chapter Two

The moment they walked through the barn's big white double doors, Dylan was hit by the familiar sweet smell of hay and grain. She inhaled deeply and, for the first time since she'd arrived, she felt really at home. *Just bring down my luggage and I'll room here!* she thought. Opening her eyes, she looked around. The barn had a wide centre aisle, lined on either side with box stalls. Most of the ponies were still out in the paddocks, but at least five horses were looking over their doors with their ears pricked, hoping for a treat. Dylan smiled at Honey and they headed down the aisle together, taking it all in.

A group of girls stood by one of the stalls, admiring a handsome blue roan pony still in travelling wraps. Dylan hesitated when she walked past. She was sure she recognized the tall blond girl who was combing her fingers through the roan's long forelock. As if she had read Dylan's mind, the girl looked over, narrowing her grey-blue eyes. Dylan frowned as she searched her recent memory to match the girl's face with a situation. At that moment the pony poked his head over the door, rattling his immaculate leather halter against the door frame. An engraved brass plaque on the cheekpiece caught the light, and Dylan squinted to read the pony's name: *Bluegrass*. She suddenly made the connection. She had met the pony's rider at a show in Rhode Island that summer. Dylan remembered the pony, but she couldn't recall the girl's name.

"Hi," the girl said. Her voice was cool but friendly. "Do we know each other?"

"Sort of. We were both at the Red Valley show last July. You were riding in the Large Pony class and I was in the Medium group. I think I loaned you some fly spray," Dylan recalled.

"Right! I remember now." The girl smiled. "You had Absorbine. It's the only brand I can use on Bluegrass. He's allergic to everything else."

Dylan nodded and smiled. The girl seemed pretty down-to-earth, but Dylan couldn't get over the fact that she was hanging out in the stable wearing a burgundy skirt-and-shirt ensemble that looked far more appropriate for a Parisian nightclub. As far as Dylan could tell, her roommate had been shocked into silence. Honey looked around at the girls with one eyebrow raised.

"Hey, guys, you've all heard the news, right?" Tanisha, the eighth-grader who had pushed past Dylan on the staircase, let herself out of a stall and walked up to the small group. The sound of a radio drifted from behind her, and Dylan heard girls chatting at the far end of the barn. Tanisha paused, making sure she had everyone's attention. "Elizabeth Mitchell left. She's going to be teaching at Allbright's this year!"

"That's old news. I hear our new Director of Riding, Ali Carmichael, is from out West," replied a girl who wore her dark brown hair in a sleek bob. "Somewhere in Kentucky."

"You've gotta be kidding, Patience," said Tanisha, opening her eyes wide. "They only turn out jockeys there!"

Kentucky isn't only for horse racing, Dylan thought, shifting her feet uncomfortably. *And it is hardly "out West."* She wondered whether she should stick up for her aunt. She didn't want to seem like she was picking fights already, but Ali deserved more credit than she was getting from the rumour mill.

The girl who had been at the Red Valley show untwisted a mint from its wrapper and fed it to Bluegrass. "I just hope she can cut it. My sister, Rachel, was the captain of the senior jumping team last year, and they won the Interscholastic championship. Rachel had nothing but praise for Elizabeth Mitchell, and now she's training our top rivals. Let's hope this new instructor doesn't think that the way to win medals is by galloping around with our stirrups too short." She gave a pretend shudder. "It'll take a lot more than speed to beat Allbright's. Kentucky might have the Derby, but Virginia is real horse country."

"You are so bad," Patience said as they all broke into laughter. "Don't worry. She won't be here long if she doesn't have what it takes. The headmistress will see to that."

Dylan felt her cheeks burn and forced herself to swallow her words. *Were they serious? How could they joke around about someone's job like that? They hadn't even met Ali yet*. Dylan knew that if she stayed a second longer, she might say something that either she or Ali would regret.

"Catch you later," Dylan announced abruptly. She turned to leave, noticing Honey glance from her to the other girls with a puzzled frown.

Dylan gritted her teeth and walked down the aisle, toward the far end of the barn, with Honey close behind. A grey mare tossed her head and pawed the floor, obviously hoping for some attention, but Dylan kept walking, scanning the stalls for Morello.

A familiar whinny greeted her from the end of the row as a handsome brown-and-white face looked out from the last stall. His forelock was standing up in a ratty tuft. Dylan guessed he'd been rubbing his head against his haynet again.

"Hello, boy." Dylan smiled. She held out her hand for Morello to smell before reaching up to pull out the strands of hay tangled in his forelock. "Up to your old habits, I see. Are you getting used to your new home?" She put her face against his neck and felt herself relax.

"Oh, he's lovely!" Honey said with an exaggerated sigh after she had stepped up to Morello's stall. "He's even cuter than his photo! You're so lucky to have your own pony here."

Dylan fumbled in her pocket for a horse cookie. Morello wasn't technically her pony, since he belonged to Ali, but she had forged such a strong bond with him over her summer visit that he felt almost as good as the real thing. Still, she wanted to be honest with Honey. She seemed nice, so Dylan figured she could trust Honey with the truth about her bond with Morello. But just as she was about to launch into the explanation, she heard another voice behind them.

"He's been looking for someone to give him some TLC all afternoon. I think he's feeling a bit homesick."

Dylan spun around to find her aunt looking at her with an uncertain expression in her brown eyes. Dylan turned bright red. *It must have sounded like I told Honey that Morello was mine*, she thought guiltily.

"I'm Ms Carmichael, Chestnut Hill's new riding instructor." Dylan's aunt wiped her hand on her breeches before holding it out to Honey.

"I'm Felicity Harper – but my friends call me Honey," Dylan's roommate explained.

"I think you've already been introduced to Morello? I brought him along with my other horse, Quince. He's across in the other stable, looking even lonelier!"

Honey darted a confused look at Dylan.

Dylan groaned inwardly. How was she going to explain this without sounding like a compulsive liar?

"Are you both settling in OK?" Ali Carmichael asked, pushing her fingers through her short dark hair.

"Great, thanks," Honey said. "The horses are gorgeous!"

Dylan didn't reply. Her mouth felt as if it had become temporarily detached from her brain. She didn't trust herself not to blurt out something else that would get her in social turmoil.

"Well, if I don't see you sooner, then I'll look forward to seeing you when classes start on Monday." Ali smiled. "If I remember my schedule correctly, I'm assessing you then, right, Honey? We'll have to see which level of the riding programme would be best for you."

Honey nodded. "I hope I make the intermediate programme. I like jumping, but I'd really love to do some work on my dressage this year."

"Well, we'll soon see if you're up to the intermediate level," Ali Carmichael said, leaning over the stall door to straighten Morello's dark blue sheet. "Don't worry, the assessment isn't too difficult. But there's no point over-stretching your skills in the first term, so I like to get a sense of where you'll learn the most. OK, then, I'll see you on Monday." She walked back up the aisle, pausing to talk to one of the seniors who was just going into the grey mare's stall.

"She seems really nice," Honey said, breaking the silence. "I hope she's up to the other girls' standards."

"Yeah," Dylan agreed absently, her eyes still following her aunt. She knew Honey must wonder why Dylan had acted like she owned Morello – and why she had a photo of the new riding instructor's pony in her room. But Dylan also knew she couldn't set Honey straight without admitting Ms Carmichael was her aunt, and that wasn't something she was ready to do yet. She had decided she wanted to be known first as Dylan Walsh at Chestnut Hill, not as Ali Carmichael's niece. She'd tell everyone eventually. By then, she was sure she'd have lots of loyal friends – and Ali would have loyal students and admirers.

"Let's go check out the other barn," she suggested over the sound of a horse's hooves approaching.

"OK." Honey nodded as she crossed the aisle to open the door of the opposite stall. "I'll get that for you," she offered to a girl who was leading a broad-faced liver chestnut.

The girl clicked her tongue and gave the pony a pat as he walked into the stall. "Hey, could you do me a favour? Can you go see if Rose's stable sheet is in the tack room? I asked for it to be put in her stall, but it's not here," she said. "You can just ask anyone in there if they've seen Paige Cox's stuff."

"We're on it," Dylan said, motioning to Honey. Dylan welcomed the chance to have a look around the tack room. She planned to know every inch of the stable yard before the weekend was over.

Dylan and Honey may have found their way around the stables without a problem, but they got lost twice in the dorm hallways before they finally made it back to their room.

"I vote we tie a ball of string to the doorknob and unravel it behind us next time we go out!" Dylan laughed, opening the door. "The horses would eat bread crumbs, so that would never work."

It took them a few seconds before they realized that their third roommate was there, filling the bulletin board with pictures of herself and a beautiful blue roan pony. She turned around, flipping her long hair over her shoulder with a practiced swish, and Dylan saw that Lynsey Harrison (a.k.a. BBB) was none other than the blond girl from the barn – the one who had questioned whether Ali Carmichael was up to the challenge of teaching at a Virginia boarding school. Lots of the girls had voiced their doubts, but Dylan felt like Lynsey's tone had been particularly harsh.

"Hi, guys! You must be my roommates. I'm Lynsey Harrison. Didn't we meet earlier?" The girl greeted them with a gush of charm and none of the attitude from the barn. Dylan still felt suspicious of the girl but was determined to put the previous conversation behind her.

"We sure did," Dylan replied, introducing herself and Honey.

"So, what do you think of it here so far?" Lynsey asked, pinning up another picture – this one of her sunbathing on a pool recliner with a magnificent white antebellum mansion in the background. "Of course, I already know the campus like the back of my hand – both my sisters went to Chestnut Hill," she continued without giving them a chance to answer.

Dylan was distracted by the sound of the door opening. Patience, the dark-haired girl they'd seen in the barn, casually strolled into the room without even knocking. "Hi," she said. She nodded at the picture of Rocky on Honey's bedside table. "I was admiring that photo a few minutes ago, wasn't I, Lynsey? He's such a cute guy! Did you bring him with you?"

"If only." Honey smiled.

"We were about to go check out the tennis courts. Why don't you come with us and tell us all about him?" Lynsey suggested, pushing a thumbtack down on the corner of a photo.

From Lynsey's detached tone, Dylan had a feeling that she wasn't all that interested in hearing why Honey hadn't been able to bring Rocky with her. Lynsey looked at Dylan. "You can come too, if you want."

"I'd be up for tennis," Honey admitted. "I loved playing back home. In fact, as a treat before we moved this summer, my dad got us all tickets for Centre Court at Wimbledon."

"You're kidding!" Lynsey said. "I really wanted to do Britain while we were yachting in the Mediterranean this summer, but my mom insisted it would be too cold to go that far north." She shrugged. "I did get some great outfits in Monaco, and we stayed at an old vineyard in Tuscany, but there wasn't enough time to go to all the places I wanted."

"So you're from England?" Patience said, looking at Honey with genuine interest in her hazel eyes. "Wow, I've always wondered what it would be like living there. There's so much history all around. Do you know Prince William?"

"No, I do have a friend at Eton, but we're much younger than either of the princes," Honey told them, looking a bit awkward.

Patience shrugged. "My dad thought about sending me to school overseas," Patience added. "Wait until I tell him that there's a British girl on my floor at Chestnut Hill."

Dylan resisted the urge to roll her eyes. Lynsey and Patience were treating Honey like she was an exhibit in a museum or a freak show. *Come and see The Incredible Walking, Talking Girl from England!*

Lynsey looked at her watch. "Hey, guys, if we're going to go try out the courts, then we need to head down now. We have less than two hours before convocation." She held open the door and then tapped her forehead with her hand. "I forgot to mention …I hope you don't mind, Dylan, but I went ahead and moved some of your stuff into your closet. It was in my way. I guess that's the problem with your bed being in the middle of the room – you'll have to be careful that you don't leave things on the floor."

Dylan looked down at the empty area around her bed and then back at Lynsey. "Or, I can just leave things out and you can put them away for me." She laughed at her own joke, but Lynsey only gave her a blank expression in return. *OK, so I guess I should lay off the sarcasm a bit*, Dylan thought.

"Are you coming with us?" Honey asked.

"I don't think so. I play tennis with two left hands," Dylan replied, making a face.

"OK. See you later," Honey said, following Lynsey and Patience out the door.

"Later," Dylan echoed. She fell back on her bed – the one in the middle of the room – and put her hands behind her head. She wondered what she should do now that she had the room to herself. She savoured the peace and quiet, guessing she might not get a lot of it with Lynsey and Patience around.

But twenty seconds later, she grabbed her paddock boots out of the closet where Lynsey had deposited them, pulled them on, took her hard hat in her hand, and headed out the door. Who needed peace and quiet when you had horses?

Chapter Three

Dylan headed straight back to the stable yard, figuring she had over an hour to acquaint herself with some of the horses. First off, she'd take a good look at Bluegrass, since Lynsey was out of the way. The blue roan was one of the classiest ponies Dylan had ever seen. His speckled dark coat gleamed, and there were threads of silver running through his long silky mane and tail.

Bluegrass swung his head around and stared past Dylan, his small ears pricked at the sound of hooves. Ali Carmichael was leading a grey pony toward her. "I'm glad you're here, Dylan," she said. There was a warmth in her voice that Dylan hadn't noticed earlier. "Can you take a halter from the tack room and bring in Nutmeg for me? She's the small buckskin in the top paddock. She didn't want to be caught earlier, the little troublemaker. It would be a big help. Kelly and Sarah need to start the evening feeds, and I have three horses to lunge before I can get ready for convocation."

"OK," Dylan said, guessing that Kelly and Sarah

must be the stable hands. She was more than happy to ease her aunt's workload. It had to be a busy day, with all the students' ponies arriving.

"The tack room is at the far end, across from Morello's stall," Ali Carmichael called over her shoulder as Dylan hurried down the aisle. If Nutmeg was tricky to catch, then she didn't want to waste any time. *I can just see myself being late to convocation after chasing a stubborn pony for an hour,* she thought. Dylan cringed at the thought. She hated being late.

She jogged along the path that led away from the barn and slowed as a girl with wavy blond hair passed, leading a palomino gelding.

She looked at the halter slung over Dylan's shoulder. "Are you going to catch Nutmeg?"

"How did you know?"

"She's the only one left. Nutmeg's really sweet most of the time and will do anything for a cookie, but sometimes she decides not to play ball…"

"Unless the game is dodgeball?" Dylan guessed.

"Exactly. And you're the ball," the girl confirmed with a laugh. "Good luck!"

"Thanks. It sounds like I'm going to need it. Are you Sarah?" Dylan asked.

"Close. I'm Kelly." She turned around and continued to lead the palomino in the direction of the stables.

Dylan tried to commit the name to memory, then looked toward the paddocks. She rolled her shoulders in circles like a boxer limbering up in the ring. "OK, Nutmeg, prepare to meet your match," she announced.

"This is one girl who doesn't take any monkey business from a pony – not even one with big-horse attitude."

She was surprised to see the buckskin mare standing just inside the gate with her head over the fence, her ears pricked forward as if she were just waiting for Dylan. As she came closer, Dylan noticed that Nutmeg had patches of dried dirt on her hindquarters. Her fingers twitched, and she wondered how soon she would be allowed to groom the ponies.

Dylan adjusted the halter so it was hidden by her arm and then climbed over the gate, talking to Nutmeg all the time. "Hello, girl. Aren't you gorgeous? Have you been rolling? How'd you get so dirty? I'll give you a good brushing if you come in. Your dinner will be waiting for you. I hear molasses is on the menu tonight." Dylan kept talking in a friendly tone as she reached into her pocket for a horse cookie. "You want a treat? Yeah, you're such a good girl – hey!"

With lightning speed, Nutmeg snatched the cookie off Dylan's palm and wheeled away at a brisk canter, kicking up her back hooves.

"Of all the rotten, ungrateful creatures," Dylan muttered as Nutmeg skidded to a halt and turned back to study her. The mare tossed her head up and down, and Dylan swore she was taunting her. She could almost hear the pony laughing.

Then Dylan realized that there was the sound of real laughter behind her. She spun around to see a girl with dark curly hair and sparkling blue eyes leaning on the gate. "I thought she was a gorgeous, good girl!"

"She obviously has a problem with authority," Dylan said with a defensive shrug, but she couldn't help laughing herself.

"Do you want a hand?" the girl offered.

"Well, I think it'll take about ten extra hands and a lasso, but if you want to give it a try, be my guest," Dylan replied. "I'm Dylan Walsh, by the way. I'm in Adams House."

"Malory O'Neil. I'm in Adams, too."

Dylan had assumed from the girl's worn jodhpurs and old yard boots that she was one of the assistants who had looked after the horses during summer vacation. She did a quick mental reassessment now that she knew Malory was a student – and dormmate. "So, do you have a plan?"

"I have an idea," Malory answered quickly as she reached out for the halter. "Come on." She flashed Dylan a smile and headed toward Nutmeg. The mare had dropped her head and was busy grazing.

Dylan guessed the pony was just pretending to concentrate on the grass. More than likely, she was watching their every move and calculating her next escape. When they were a short distance away, Malory paused and tucked the halter under her shirt. "Do you mind if I try something a little odd?"

"Go for it," Dylan urged, wondering what Malory had in mind. "I'm not sure anything less than a tranquilizer dart is going to work. That pony could teach Houdini a thing or two!"

Malory gave a low laugh. "Well, here goes nothing."

Dylan watched in amazement as Malory dropped onto all fours and began to crawl toward the paddock gate. Nutmeg's curiosity was obvious. The pony stopped chewing to watch Malory's small, hunched body move across the ground. *She looks like a giant turtle*, Dylan thought, biting back a grin. She had no clue how Malory thought she would catch Nutmeg by slithering in the opposite direction. Still, no matter how funny Malory looked, she had gotten Nutmeg's attention. The pony took a couple of hesitant steps, following Malory's path.

Go, Malory! Dylan gave a silent cheer when Nutmeg began to follow Malory in earnest, stretching out her neck as she got closer. At last, her muzzle bumped against Malory's back as the pony sniffed with curiosity. Then, very quickly, with smooth, gentle movements so Nutmeg wouldn't be frightened, Malory reached her arm around the mare's neck and pulled the halter over her ears, then securely clipped the strap.

Dylan let out a yell and jogged over to join them. "That was totally amazing – where did you learn that trick?"

Malory rubbed Nutmeg on the swirl between her eyes before leading the mare to the gate. "My old riding instructor showed it to me," she explained. "Where I learned to ride, we had to catch and tack up our own ponies. The trainer said it was an important part of learning stable management. I rode this horse named Ivan for a while. He refused to be caught, but he could never resist the crawling trick."

"I could have used that one in Connecticut!" Dylan admitted. "We had some stubborn ponies there, too, but none as wily as Nutmeg." She gave the buckskin a light pat on the neck. "Where did you learn to ride?"

Malory clicked to Nutmeg to walk up the path and seemed to hesitate before saying, "Cheney Falls Stables."

"So you live close by?" Dylan asked, recognizing the name of the town just west of Chestnut Hill. "Does that mean you're a day student?"

Malory shook her head. "No, I'm boarding. In Adams."

"Oh, that's right. You said that. Sorry." Dylan glanced over at Malory and got the impression she didn't want to say any more. Dylan decided to keep quiet so Malory would have the chance to open up if she wanted to, but the other girl stayed silent. Malory just concentrated on twisting the end of the lead rope around her fingers, her brown curls falling forward into her face. Dylan wondered if it had been something she'd said, but then she chalked it up to first-day jitters. *Besides*, she thought, *it's kind of nice to just walk with someone and not have to chitchat the whole time.*

The buckskin mare walked faster when she saw the barn, obviously anxious to get her nose into the promised bucket of molasses. At that moment, Ali Carmichael strode out through the double doors. "Great, you caught her," she smiled.

"Yeah, thanks to Malory," Dylan said. She didn't want to take credit for Malory's triumph – especially since Ali had already overheard her pretty much telling Honey that Morello was her very own.

"Good work," said Ali. "I'm glad you've met, since you'll be in the intermediate riding programme together."

"Cool!" Dylan said enthusiastically. She hadn't been absolutely sure she'd get into the intermediate programme, although she'd crossed her fingers when her mom had filled out the application. The intermediate programme had separate modules for dressage, show jumping, and cross-country, using the professionally built course that ran through the back hills of the Chestnut Hill campus. There was also a brief unit when the girls had a chance to try different kinds of riding, like sidesaddle and Western. Dylan couldn't wait!

"Would either of you mind helping me out a little more?" Ali asked, taking Nutmeg's lead rope. "Colorado and Kingfisher still haven't been exercised today. I was going to lunge them, but if you could tack them up and bring them down to the ring, I could give you both a quick lesson. It will be just for a half hour on the flat – we can't risk being late for convocation – but it would be fun."

"I'm in!" Dylan said, exchanging a smile with Malory.

Ali pulled off her old blue sweatshirt as the sun came out from behind a cloud. "Dylan, I'd like to see how you go on Colorado. You'll have your work cut out for you, because he can be a bit of a mule. Malory, you take Kingfisher. I'll meet you down in the outdoor arena."

Dylan and Malory grabbed the horses' tack from the clearly labeled hooks before separating outside the stall doors.

"Hey, Colorado," Dylan said, pulling back the bolt. The handsome dun gelding ambled through the deep bed of straw toward her. His coat gleamed, and Dylan could see that she wouldn't have to groom him. Before tacking up, she held out her hand for him to sniff. The gelding lipped hopefully at her palm, flicking his ears back when he discovered that there was no treat.

"Maybe later, if you behave yourself," Dylan said with a laugh, slipping the reins over his head. Her spirits picked up when Colorado willingly opened his mouth for the bit and she neatly buckled the bridle on. *If only you were Morello, then this day would be perfect!* But she was only half-serious. It was always fun riding a new pony, and Dylan was sure she and Morello would have their proper reunion soon.

"I'm all set. Are you ready?" Malory called over the adjoining partition wall.

"Sheesh, what have you got, six hands?" Dylan called back.

Malory laughed. "No, just two, but they move very quickly."

Dylan grinned and hurriedly slid Colorado's saddle onto his back. By the time she was ready, Malory had already led Kingfisher out and was mounted on the pretty bay.

40

Dylan checked her girth before swinging lightly onto Colorado's back and clicking her tongue for him to walk on. They fell in alongside Kingfisher and made their way to the outdoor arena. The first thing Dylan noticed was that Colorado had a much shorter stride than she was used to, and she had a feeling that she'd have to use her legs and seat strongly to get him to respond well.

Ali Carmichael was waiting for them in the centre of the arena. She gave the girls a quick wave. Dylan thought her aunt looked right at home – her tall, lean figure made her seem commanding and confident. "OK, spread out and trot a serpentine, please," Ali called.

Kingfisher burst into a lively trot, and Dylan waited a few moments and then, with a squeeze, asked Colorado to trot. Immediately, the gelding stiffened and raised his head in protest. *Oh, no, you don't*, Dylan thought. She tightened her legs until the gelding broke into a slow trot, but for the entire serpentine he resisted Dylan's hand and leg signals, making it clear that he would rather be back in his stall.

"Bring them to a walk and come into the centre!" Ali called after they had finished three loops. "You had Kingfisher going nicely, Malory. You rode him very sympathetically considering it's the first time you've been on him." She smiled. "But I'd like to see him be a little more responsive. I'd like you to use half-halts – light squeezes on the reins – so you have him really listening to you, OK?"

"Sure," Malory nodded, patting Kingfisher's neck.

"Dylan." Ali turned to her, reaching up to pull Colorado's black forelock free from his browband. "Colorado's not working for you. You have to use your seat and a lot more leg to get him to respond. He's not a push-button pony. He requires a strong rider. If you want to get him to go for you, you've got to give one hundred percent."

Dylan stared at her aunt. *Feel free to tell it like it is,* she thought. *Don't be easy on me because we're related. No, don't sugarcoat it to spare my feelings.* Dylan wondered why Ali had to be so harsh. She'd had no problem praising Malory. Dylan hadn't been on Colorado more than four minutes. Ali hadn't even given her a chance!

"I want you drop your stirrups and trot him in a small circle at the far end," her aunt finished, stepping back.

Malory gave Dylan a sympathetic look as she rode past. Dylan made a face, hoping Malory wouldn't notice how frustrated she was. She twisted her ankles to dig her heels into Colorado.

"Make sure your signals are invisible," Ali called.

Luckily, Dylan's back was to her aunt, so she could roll her eyes as dramatically as she liked. At least she could put her frustration to good use by squeezing Colorado. She soon found that, to get the reluctant pony on the bit, she had to use her legs for every stride. She lost count of the number of times they circled, and her legs began to burn. Biting her lower lip, she felt a rush of delight when the gelding finally lowered his head and began to bring his quarters underneath him. *Good boy!* Suddenly the short, lazy stride felt powerful, and Dylan grinned, forgetting all about her aching legs.

"OK, Dylan, come in," Ali called over her shoulder. Malory was cantering Kingfisher at the other end of the ring, and Ali's attention seemed to be totally focused on her. Feeling a little frustrated, Dylan uncrossed her stirrups and patted Colorado's damp neck before walking him into the centre of the arena on a long rein. She had to admit that Malory had Kingfisher going in a beautiful, collected canter. Malory sat lightly in the saddle, supple at the waist to accommodate Kingfisher's long, bouncy stride, and her hands were completely still. Malory was much taller than Dylan, and her long legs added an elegant quality to her riding position. When she finally slowed Kingfisher to a trot, her cheeks were flushed and her eyes sparkling.

"You were right, Ms Carmichael! The half-halts really made him listen!" she exclaimed.

"You did great," Ali told her.

"Dylan had Colorado working well, too." Malory smiled across at Dylan.

"Yes." Dylan's aunt nodded. "You got him to go on the bit, but you need to use your inside leg more to help him bend inward on the corners." Once again, all Dylan could do was give her aunt a dull stare. With one sentence, Ali had erased all of her positive feelings about her work with Colorado. She wasn't sure what to say in reply. She certainly didn't want to be too meek and agree with every single thing that Ali said – Malory was already doing enough of that for both of them.

Dylan felt her cheeks burn with guilt for trying to place blame on Malory. She looked down and fiddled with a piece of Colorado's mane.

"I think that's enough for today. Walk a few laps to cool them off and then take them back in," Ali Carmichael instructed. "Don't forget that you have to change into uniform for convocation."

Dylan let the reins slip through her fingers so that Colorado was able to stretch his neck.

"It's nice to see you riding again." At first Dylan thought her aunt was talking to her, but as she glanced back she saw that Ali had her hand on Kingfisher's shoulder and was looking up at Malory.

Dylan turned to face forward again and frowned. *Malory must have ridden at Chestnut Hill at some point during the summer. How else would Aunt Ali have seen her ride?* It made sense, if Malory lived close by. Under normal circumstances, Dylan would have just asked Malory, but she remembered how reticent the girl had been earlier.

She couldn't help but be curious, but for now she had to hurry and untack. She only had twenty minutes until convocation – the official start of the school year!

Chapter Four

Dylan pulled her grey jacket on over the navy blue sweater and then glanced across at Honey. "Is that how they wear uniforms back in England?" She nodded at the price tag still hanging off Honey's sleeve. "Or are you trying to start a new trend? I don't really think it will catch on."

Honey glanced down at her sleeve. "Yikes! I can't believe I missed that!"

"I think there's a pair of scissors in my cosmetics bag," Dylan told her, starting to rummage in her nightstand.

"It's OK, I'm already on it." Lynsey had finished getting changed and was looking ultrasmart in her uniform, which somehow seemed better tailored than anyone else's. *How come I look like a girl in an oversized blazer and she looks like something out of an early Britney Spears video?* Dylan wondered. She wouldn't have been surprised if Lynsey had her own personal fashion designer and tailor based in a wing of her sprawling white mansion. She felt like she knew the Harrisons' home better than her own after seeing the photo collage of the Harrison estate that covered the shared bulletin board.

Lynsey took a suede manicure case over to Honey. "There you go," she said, neatly snipping off the label and tossing it in the wastepaper basket.

"Let's go." Dylan took one final look in the full-length mirror to check out her appearance, taking a second glance as she noticed a strand of hay in her hair. "Thanks, you guys – you were going to let me cruise into convocation with half a bale of hay in my hair," she said.

"I thought you were trying to start a new trend," Honey said, straight-faced.

Dylan groaned. "Fine, I guess I deserved that one."

"Seriously, Dylan," Honey assured her. "I didn't see it. I would have told you if I did."

Dylan couldn't help but smile. Honey was so sincere.

"Are you ready yet?" Lynsey glanced at her Cartier watch and stepped into the hallway.

Dylan bent over and shook her head, running her hands through her hair. She flipped her head back and grabbed the doorknob. "Wait up!" she yelled down the corridor. "I'm right behind you!"

They joined the groups of Chestnut Hill girls filing into the chapel through the massive arched wooden doors. The chapel was over a hundred years old and had a musty charm. The late-afternoon sunshine peeked through tall stained-glass windows, and pools of dazzling colour danced like a giant kaleidoscope on the oak floorboards and polished pews. Dylan followed Honey and Lynsey toward the front rows, where the rest of the seventh-graders were seated. She straightened up when she noticed that the faculty members were already in place, sitting at the top of the sanctuary in pews that faced into the centre of the chapel. She scanned the solemn faces until she found her aunt, who was on the end of one of the wooden benches, dressed in the same ceremonial black gown as the rest of the staff.

From the second row, Patience turned her head and motioned with a lift of her chin for Lynsey to sit beside her. Dylan bit her lip as she looked at the minimal space left on the bench. "We'll all fit," Lynsey announced, sliding down. "Scoot over some, OK, Patience?"

Sure enough, Honey and Dylan settled into the pew. Dylan crossed her ankles and took a deep breath. Almost immediately Lynsey gave a snort of laughter. "Check out the chic footwear on our esteemed Director of Riding," she whispered to Patience.

Patience peered at Ali Carmichael from under her lashes, and Dylan followed her gaze to see her aunt's dirty rubber boots poking out from underneath the shiny black gown. "Oh, they are sooo this season," Patience whispered back.

Dylan dug her fingernails into her palms. *Way to give*

them ammunition, Aunt Ali. Even though she was still simmering with frustration from the lesson, Dylan still wished her aunt hadn't made herself such an easy target. Did she have any clue where she was? Dylan knew her aunt was laid back, but at least she could try to make an effort. As she shook her head, Dylan could feel Honey looking at her and didn't dare meet her glance.

"Where do you think I could get a pair?" Patience went on.

"Hicksville," Lynsey replied without missing a beat.

Dylan shifted uncomfortably as the muffled laughter traveled from girl to girl.

The whispers faded at the sound of footsteps echoing from the vaulted ceiling. The rows all turned in slightly to watch the principal, Dr Angela Starling, walk down the centre aisle. The sunlight highlighted glints of red in her long dark hair, which was swept up into a French twist. Her black gown flared with each long stride. She climbed the slate stairs into the pulpit and opened the heavy book resting on the antique lectern. Instead of reading from the book, she glanced up to smile at the seated girls. Her eyes swept over the sanctuary, and Dylan had the distinct feeling that the principal was looking directly at her.

"Welcome! I'm very pleased to be greeting you at the start of a new year at Chestnut Hill." Her voice was low and melodious but still carried to the back of the chapel. "Before I give a reading, I'd like to welcome our new seventh-graders." An excited murmur ran through the rows, and Dylan felt a fizz of exhilaration at the thought of being a Chestnut Hill student for the next six years. Even the minor setbacks of the day couldn't take that feeling away. She glanced up at the wall behind Dr Starling, where impressive maple plaques hung from the exposed beams. Long lists of scholars and academics who had attended Chestnut Hill were engraved in gold italic letters. Dylan didn't know why Lynsey and Patience were so hung up on English history and culture. There was more than enough history and tradition right here at Chestnut Hill!

"As you know, we have the highest standards at Chestnut Hill. As Virginia's oldest all-girl institution, we must strive for excellence in all our pursuits. Just by the fact that you are seated in this chapel, I know each of you has proven you have what it takes to make a lasting contribution to Chestnut Hill – and beyond." Dr Starling paused before continuing.

"It's true that there is a lot to live up to at Chestnut Hill, yet this does not necessarily mean you should tread in the footsteps of those who have gone before. Each one of you will distinguish yourself in your own way. And it is our job, as the faculty of Chestnut Hill, to help you discover what you have to offer." Dr Starling's grey eyes twinkled, and Dylan wondered how the principal had known just what to say to both comfort and inspire her. "Before we sing our first hymn, I'd like to welcome the newest member of our faculty, Ms Ali Carmichael. Knowing the way news spreads around campus, I'm sure that many of you have already heard that she has replaced our previous Director of Riding, Elizabeth Mitchell." Dr Starling smiled. "We have a fine tradition of equestrianism here at Chestnut Hill and I have no doubt that Ms Carmichael is going to ensure that our riding teams continue to excel and, more importantly, that we don't let the Interscholastic Championship cup fall into the hands of Allbright Academy this year!"

Some of the seniors at the back of the hall let out a small cheer, and Dr Starling smiled again.

"There's more good news regarding our equestrian achievements," Dr Starling went on. "For the first time in seven years, we have a first-year student who has been awarded the prestigious Rockwell Award." Dylan felt Lynsey tense beside her and there was an outbreak of curious whispers. Honey raised her eyebrows inquiringly, but Dylan shook her head. She had never even heard of the Rockwell Award.

"I bet it's Lynsey Harrison," a girl murmured directly behind them. "She was champion at three A-level shows this year."

Dylan bit back a grin. *Somehow, I have a feeling that if Lynsey had won something, we'd know about it by now*, she thought.

"Fifteen years ago, Diane Rockwell represented the United States in the Olympic Games, and she's always insisted she owes everything to the riding instruction she received here at Chestnut Hill. She set up the generous grant to enable other girls to achieve their ambitions. Her grant has two essential qualifications:

the recipient should have above-average talent and be just a little bit horse-crazy." Dr Starling reached for a glass of water on the lectern and took a sip. "I would like to extend a special welcome to this year's winner of the Rockwell Award, Malory O'Neil."

Most of the girls in the chapel started craning their necks, trying to figure out which of the girls in the seventh-grade seating section was Malory. Dylan leaned forward and looked at the girl who was sitting at the end of her pew. Malory sat motionless, her eyes down and her cheeks bright red. Dylan guessed the award explained why her aunt had seen Malory ride before, but why hadn't Malory told her about the scholarship in the stable? If it had been her, Dylan wouldn't have been able to keep quiet about it! Maybe Malory hadn't wanted to sound like she was bragging, but Dylan couldn't imagine her coming off as arrogant.

"I never noticed her on the circuit, and I rode in all of the A-level shows in Virginia this summer," Lynsey whispered to Dylan. "I'd love to know how she managed to catch Ms Rockwell's eye, because I didn't see her."

Dylan shrugged. "Maybe she wasn't riding in the big shows."

"Then how did she win the award?" Lynsey shot back. "Unless she was on the Florida winter circuit – that's the only explanation." Dylan was relieved she didn't have to reply, because Dr Starling had announced their first hymn. The organ struck the opening chords, and Dylan took the hymn sheet that

Honey passed down from the end of the row. As she stood up to sing the first line, Dylan's heart swelled along with the raised voices. She was happy that Malory had snagged the prestigious award. Although she had to admit that she'd have been happy for anyone to receive it other than Lynsey; it was only the first day, but Dylan was already getting a little bored with her roommate's endless self-promotion. She could tell that there was going to be some fierce competition for the junior jumping team – and she hadn't even met any of the other intermediate programme students yet!

Dylan hovered in the entrance of the middle school sitting room, smoothing her new Juicy Couture hooded sweatshirt. She chewed her bottom lip, wishing that she hadn't taken so long choosing between her hoodie and her sleeveless Fossil top. She had told Lynsey and Honey that she'd catch up with them, but she hadn't anticipated being the last one to arrive in the lounge.

"Dylan!" There was a shout from the far end of the room and Dylan saw Honey stand up and wave.

At the end of convocation, Dr Starling had announced that, as a treat, all the girls would have pizza for dinner in their separate dorms. Usually the boarders would eat together in the student centre cafeteria, but having their evening meal in the common rooms would give the dormmates a chance to get to know one another.

Dylan sat down on the cranberry-coloured sofa beside Lynsey and Honey. Patience was sitting on the facing sofa with two girls whom Dylan had noticed in the chapel. To Dylan's right, Malory was seated on a high-back chair with one leg tucked beneath her, and a girl wearing stylish rimless glasses was on the matching ottoman.

"This is Wei Lin Chang," Patience explained, turning from Lynsey to the petite girl beside her.

"Hi there," Wei Lin said and smiled, revealing a mouthful of perfect white teeth. Her shiny black hair was cut into a sleek chin-length bob. "How are you doing?"

"And I'm Razina Jackson," said the other girl on Patience's sofa. "We're all in Adams Four. Nice to meet you." Her braided black hair swung down over her shoulder as she leaned across the low table to shake hands. Dylan was impressed with Razina's presence – she made a point of looking everyone in the eye as she offered her hand. She seemed so mature, Dylan wondered what her story was. The others all took their cue from Razina and introduced themselves. The girl with the rimless glasses, turned out to be Malory's roommate, Alexandra Cooper.

"We're still waiting for Lani, our other roomie, to arrive," Alexandra added, pushing her glasses up her nose.

Dylan looked around at all the girls and wondered how she was going to remember the names. And this was just the first-year students in Adams. There were five other houses!

"Your last name sounds familiar," Wei Lin told Patience. "Are you from the Boston area?"

"My father is Edward Hunter Duvall," Patience said. She flicked her light brown hair over her shoulder and sounded bored, as if she'd been asked this a dozen times. "You know, the novelist?"

"Oh, wow!" Wei Lin snapped her fingers in the air. "That's amazing! I love his books! Do you think the English teacher could get him to give a symposium on writing?"

"I guess I could ask him," Patience said. She still sounded offhand, but Dylan noticed a subtle smile stretch across her mouth, as if she were enjoying the attention. Dylan thought the name Edward Duvall sounded familiar, but she had never read anything by him.

"So, Malory," Lynsey said, leaning forward to take a carrot stick from the coffee table. "You must have been totally excited when you got the news about the Rockwell Award. When did you find out?" She smiled at Malory before popping the carrot into her mouth.

Malory glanced up from picking at a loose thread on the cushion on her lap. "It came in the mail. Maybe in July," she recalled. "I was stunned. I thought it was my dad's idea of a joke when I opened up the letter."

"Is everyone here totally obsessed with horses?" Patience asked.

"Not me," Razina said, pouring seltzer into the glasses.

"Me, either." Wei Lin shrugged. "It's not something that's ever appealed to me. I'm more into the winter sports scene – skiing and snowboarding. Although I play tennis, too, so I'll probably try out for that."

"Hey, I love skiing!" Razina beamed. "Every Christmas my mom takes me to the Alps for a week, on our way back from Tanzania."

Dylan took a sip of the fizzy water and looked at Razina. "Wow! It sounds like you've travelled a lot!"

Razina nodded. "Yeah, I'm really lucky. My mom owns a gallery specializing in South African art and cultural relics. She homeschooled me for the last two years, so I went with her when she scouted new sources. It was an amazing experience." Somehow, Razina didn't sound at all boastful, just impassioned.

"Pizza's here!" Mrs Herson walked into the room, followed by a girl Dylan hadn't seen before. Their housemother was carrying four enormous flat boxes, and as the smell of melted cheese and oregano wafted over, Dylan realized she was licking her lips. Mrs Herson put two of the boxes down on the table beside the eighth-graders and then headed toward their group, artfully balancing their boxes on one palm.

"Ta da!" Mrs Herson spun the boxes around on her hand before sliding them neatly onto the table. Dylan suspected that the housemother had some deep-dish pizzeria experience somewhere on her résumé. The seventh-graders laughed and burst into applause. Mrs Herson grinned and waited for the noise to die away before turning to the tall girl standing next to her. "Everyone, I'd like you to say hello to Lani Hernandez from Colorado." Lani smiled at them, her freckled nose crinkling. "I'm sure they'll all introduce themselves to you," Mrs Herson added.

"How are you doing?" Lani grinned around, looking not at all fazed by her late entrance. *She looks pretty cool*, Dylan thought, taking in the girl's short dark fringe and warm brown eyes. She was wearing a long-sleeved T-shirt with a Canadian maple leaf design and slim-fitting jeans that covered all but the toe of her tan cowboy boots. "I missed my connecting flight in Chicago, but it looks like I've arrived in time for the most important part of the day." She eyed the pizzas appreciatively.

"I'm sure the girls will give you a rundown on what you missed at convocation," said Mrs Herson. "If you need any other help, my apartment is at the far end of your floor. And, everyone, don't forget that you can always go to Ms Sebastian and Mrs Marshall, the assistant and high school housemothers, if I'm not available. Their rooms are on the second floor."

Lani nodded and waited for Mrs Herson to go before taking a seat right on the floor. She rubbed her hands together and looked around the group. "Is it every woman for herself or is someone going to hand out some slices? I'm so hungry I could eat a whole cow!"

"What? You didn't bring one along with you from the ranch?" Lynsey asked sweetly. Beside her, Patience swallowed a giggle.

"Heck no!" Lani responded with an exaggerated western twang. "I tried to get me one of those steers onto the plane, but nothing doin'." Lani finished by slapping her knee.

Dylan was in the middle of taking a drink and, as she sputtered with laughter, it went down the wrong way. It was a relief to know that someone else actually had a sense of humour!

"Are you OK?" Lani asked.

"Fine, thanks." Dylan coughed as Honey hit her gently on the back.

"That's kind of a mixed blessing. If you'd choked, it would have meant extra slices for the rest of us," Lani teased.

By now Razina was handing around plates with giant slices of Hawaiian pizza.

"Delicious," Dylan sighed, taking a huge bite and dribbling some cheese down her chin.

"We were just wondering if *everyone* here is into horses," Wei Lin said. She raised her eybrows at Lani. "Don't tell me you're also going to be camping out in the barn?"

The newcomer dropped her pizza slice onto her plate to hold up her hands in mock surrender. "Guilty as charged."

"Did you ride Western where you live?" Malory asked.

Lani nodded enthusiastically. "It's pretty much all I've ridden since moving out to Colorado. My dad's a commander in the air force, so we move around a lot. I've done some English riding, too, so I'm hoping that I'll get into the intermediate programme. I have to try out or something."

"I'm being assessed for that as well," Honey said, leaning forward to pick up her drink from the table.

"No kidding! Are you nervous?" Lani asked.

"A little," Honey confessed. "I had this dream last night where I showed up at the tryout wearing my pyjamas. And then, when I looked down, I was riding a billy goat!"

"That's fabulous!" Lani announced. "I have this book on the symbolism in dreams. We have to look up the meaning of goats."

Honey gave Lani a sweet yet uncertain smile and took another bite of pizza.

Lynsey left her seat next to Dylan and squeezed in next to Patience. They immediately began discussing a party that Lynsey's grandfather, a senator in Washington, had held that summer. Wei Lin moved over to make room for Lynsey without breaking from her intent conversation with Razina, which sounded like it was about a safari.

Looking around the room, Dylan noticed everyone seemed to be involved in an animated discussion. Meeting new people was usually easy for Dylan, but for some reason she was content to eat her pizza and observe. She realized she had known a lot of girls like Lynsey and Patience back home – social, sophisticated, assertive. Some of those girls were her closest friends. *But minus the claws and cattiness*, Dylan told herself. Thinking of them, her mind drifted to the going-away party her mom had thrown for Dylan and all her riding friends. Each girl had received an unmarked box, and they all opened them on cue, releasing hundreds of gloriously coloured butterflies. Mrs Walsh had explained that the butterflies represented the group of friends: each one would take a different course – each one was beautiful and vibrant. Dylan lingered on the thought of her old friends, and when she shook herself back into the present, she realized Malory was smiling at her. Then Malory turned back to Alexandra, who was talking about their syllabus for English that year. It appeared that Alexandra had done the literature reading in its entirety over the summer.

"I loved *To Kill a Mockingbird*," Alexandra enthused.

"Wait, you've already read it?" Malory asked.

OK, Dylan thought, looking around the room in an attempt to assess the friendship possibilities. *Here's what I've got to work with in Adams. . .*

Lynsey is no doubt the queen bee – she has zero competition. It couldn't hurt to chum up with her. But not if it's too much work. You can't forget she's got a great pony – extra points for that.

I'm not so sure about Patience. It looks like she's staked a claim on Lynsey's right side, so they might come as a pre–packaged pair. And Patience is quick with the cut-downs – maybe too quick. Still, she's a little like Jess from back home, who was a super loyal friend.

Now Razina's totally together and therefore totally intimidating. But I don't think she means to be. She'll probably claim one best friend and be on the fringe of the in-crew – that's what the mature ones always do.

Wei Lin is trickier. She might be a little too smart for me. But straightforward, which is good. And pretty genuine, I think. Great sense of style. No riding.

Malory seems pretty cool. She won the Rockwell Award

– good credentials for a friend – which will impress my mom, no doubt. A little quiet, but still quirky. Kind of a suck-up to Aunt Ali, though.

Alexandra is way too smart for me. Talking about classes on the first day? No way. Nice, though.

Honey. As sweet as her name. Roommate. Rides. English. Probably thinks I'm a compulsive liar, yet still seems to like me. She has potential.

Lani – a shining beacon of hope in the humour department. Way goofy and pretty oblivious. Definite contender.

Dylan couldn't remember the last time she had been in this situation – new place, all new people. Even when she started kindergarten, she already had friends from play groups and preschool. *This is definitely new territory*, she realized, but she was up for the challenge.

When Dylan finally emerged from her character evaluations, Alexandra was still talking about English class and worrying about the caliber of the instructor.

"If it's Ms Conroy, then we'll be quoting whole acts from Shakespeare before the week is out," Lynsey said, overhearing them and breaking off her conversation with Patience. "Some of the teachers here are totally obsessed with their subjects. Ms Conroy is definitely one of them. The phys ed teacher, Ms Feist, is an absolute taskmaster. There practically has to be a hurricane before she'll cancel an outdoor practice."

"How do you know all this?" Razina licked her fingers as she finished her pizza slice.

"My sisters went here," Lynsey told her. "They gave me the full rundown."

"So tell us what the housemothers are like. Will we be able to get away with sneaking out for midnight feasts?" Lani's brown eyes sparkled and Dylan realized she had settled into the group more quickly than any of them, given that she'd only arrived ten minutes ago.

Lynsey smoothed out a wrinkle in her lilac Dolce skirt and looked around to make sure she had everyone's attention. "For one thing, don't be fooled by Mrs Herson being so laid back today. She can be fun, but be careful. There's definitely a line that you don't want to cross. The high school housemother, Ms Marshall, is the opposite. She's an absolute ogre if you break any of the house rules. She won't hesitate to report an infraction to Dr Starling."

There was a collective murmur of dread, and Lynsey paused.

"But it's fine, because she sleeps like Rip Van Winkle. After nine o'clock, anything goes. We should all pity anyone in Meyer. Mrs O'Connor wakes up at the slightest noise *and* does random night patrols. She should get a life." Lynsey's steely blue eyes flashed with disdain. "And everyone knows that the Curie dorm has the best deal with Ms Ford. They could burn down the house before she'd interfere. We need to make some friends there, so they can host parties!" Lynsey finally ran out of steam and leaned forward to take a sip of seltzer.

Dylan picked up her own drink and eyed Lynsey. The girl did talk a lot, but she sometimes shared valuable information.

Chapter Five

Chapter Five

"See you in study hall," Dylan called to Razina as she stuffed her Spanish books into her bag. Her first official riding lesson was next, and she was ready to run all the way to the stables. Razina waved as she headed in the opposite direction, toward the sports centre.

Honey and Lani were looking pretty nervous when Dylan caught up with them. Their assessment for the intermediate programme was in the indoor ring with Ali, while the riders already in the programme had a lesson in the large outdoor arena with Aiden Phillips, the jumping coach.

"You'll be great," Dylan told them. "I'll come find you if we finish early."

"Oh, fabulous. The more public the humiliation, the better," Lani said. "Do you know how long it's been since I sat in an English saddle? I'll be lucky if I can bend my knees."

"Well, if you can't, at least it will help me look better," Honey offered with a smirk.

Dylan smiled, happy to see that Honey was feeling relaxed enough to joke about the tryout. "You'll both be great," she confirmed. Then, on seeing the group of girls gathering for the intermediate lesson, she felt her own stomach flutter with nerves.

Dylan had been disappointed when Kelly, the stable assistant, had announced the pony assignments. She wasn't sure she could wait much longer to ride Morello again. *At least I'm not stuck with lazy, cranky Colorado*, she thought. Dylan had to admit that Shamrock, a fourteen-hand dappled grey mare, already seemed more willing.

When Dylan trotted into the outdoor arena, Aiden Phillips was standing in the middle watching each girl as she flashed past. "Relax, everyone, this is not a firing squad," she said. "Soften your lower back and straighten through the shoulders."

Dylan allowed herself a small smile. Straight to work – she liked it that way.

"Trot a figure eight, please," called Ms Phillips. "Malory, you cross first when you reach the far corner."

Malory looked just as natural on Flight, a pretty pure-grey mare, as she had on Kingfisher. When she reached the corner of the school, she turned straight across the ring, followed by the other riders.

Dylan changed the rein, keeping one pony-length behind Lynsey on Bluegrass, and sat for two strides to switch diagonals. Shamrock continued to trot smoothly, her head arched to accept light contact on the bit. Dylan found herself relaxing. Shamrock might not be Morello, but she moved like she was floating on air, with a smooth, even stride. This was what Dylan had been waiting for since fourth grade, and it was just day one.

Dylan fanned her cheeks with both hands as she walked away from the stable block with Malory and Lynsey. Even though it was late afternoon, the sun was still beating down. She was feeling good about her first lesson, and she guessed the other two were as well. From what she'd seen so far, Malory and Lynsey would offer the most competition among the new class for the junior riding team. Dylan knew she had a good chance, too. Except for one glaring mistake, her last round of jumps had been perfect. "I thought I was going to hit the dirt when Shamrock ran out at the oxer!" She sighed.

"You looked like a stunt rider, dangling over her shoulder like that," Lynsey agreed.

"Gee, thanks," Dylan said, giving Lynsey a gracious smile. "I'm so glad to have provided the afternoon entertainment."

Lynsey shrugged. "Oh, come on. We needed some livening up. That course was so basic, Bluegrass could have done it blindfolded."

"And with you reading a copy of *Vogue*, no doubt," Dylan said sarcastically.

"Exactly," Lynsey replied with a sly smile.

Dylan looked at Lynsey in surprise. Were they suddenly swapping jokes? She considered the possibility for a moment. It was true that Lynsey and Bluegrass were in a class of their own, not even rapping a single fence in the lesson. Lynsey could probably read the entire *Encyclopedia Britannica* without missing a stride. But Dylan was more intrigued by Lynsey's reaction to her joke. If Lynsey had somehow developed the ability to laugh at herself, she would be a lot more fun to be around.

"Since we've finished early, do you want to go down to the indoor arena to see if Lani and Honey are still doing their assessment?" Malory interrupted.

"Oh, I promised Patience I'd meet up with her once we finished," Lynsey told her. Patience was doing the basic riding programme, which had a session with Roger Musgrave, the equitation coach. "I guess I'll have to catch up with you guys later."

"Later," Dylan said, and Malory gave a quick wave.

As they headed down to the indoor ring, Sarah passed them, leading Bluegrass.

"Bluegrass is an amazing pony," Malory enthused. He looked gorgeous, his dark coat gleaming after being sprayed down to get the sweat off. "I loved watching him in today's lesson."

"But you've seen him before, right?" Dylan asked. "On the show circuit?" She had discounted Lynsey's comment about never having seen Malory at the best shows. After getting to know her better, Dylan realized it was a miracle Lynsey had remembered her from Rhode Island – and that was only because of the freakishly big flies at the Red Valley showground.

Dylan was convinced that Malory would have to have been competing a lot to win the Rockwell grant.

There was such a long pause that Dylan thought Malory wasn't even going to answer her. Finally, she lifted her hands, palms up. "I guess we must have been in different classes."

Dylan felt a twinge of annoyance. *There she goes again! Why does she always clam up the moment I ask about anything personal?*

They had reached the indoor arena and saw that the big double entrance doors were closed. They walked around to the long side of the building, to a smaller entrance that led up to the viewing gallery.

Ali Carmichael was standing in the centre of the ring, watching Honey and Lani ride at a collected trot. Dylan recognized the pony Honey was riding as they thudded past. It was Hardy, who was stabled beside Morello in the barn. Honey looked relaxed as she sat deeply in the saddle. As usual, she looked immaculate. Dylan smiled. Only Honey would wear a pressed show shirt with an overcollar for the assessment. With her cordovan-coloured gloves, beige jodhpurs, and polished boots, it was clear that Honey wanted to be taken seriously.

Lani was riding a horse that Dylan hadn't seen before, a pretty chestnut mare that looked to be about fifteen hands.

"That's Skylark," Malory whispered. "I saw Kelly schooling her yesterday, and she was being a real handful."

Dylan nodded. Skylark didn't exactly seem to be giving Lani an easy ride, either. She sidestepped along the edge of the ring with her tail kinked high. Lani drove her forward, the tassels on her chaps bouncing against her legs. Dylan didn't think that either Honey or Lani had noticed them, but as they both turned the far corner and began riding down to the mirrored end, Lani stuck her tongue out of the corner of her mouth and rolled her eyes.

Dylan turned at the sound of footsteps coming up the stairs. She scooted farther down the bench as Patience and Lynsey joined them.

"Oh, my gosh," Lynsey whispered, leaning forward and resting her elbows on the balcony. "Check out Annie Oakley."

Dylan winced. She had thought it was kind of cool that Lani was wearing chaps.

"OK, that's enough," Ali Carmichael called out to Honey and Lani.

Honey brought Hardy to a halt and leaned forward to pat his neck. When Lani tried to halt Skylark, the chestnut snatched at the bit and shot forward into a canter. The horse dropped her head, but Lani leaned back and closed her long legs against her, crossing one rein over her neck while giving and taking with the other. When Skylark came galloping around the corner, Malory gasped and closed her eyes.

"It's OK, she's still on," Dylan told her.

Lani started turning Skylark in decreasing circles, until the mare returned to a collected trot. Ali called,

"Finish off with a serpentine, please, to show her you're the one in control."

"Talk about the Wild West!" Patience murmured.

Dylan ignored her and clapped when Lani finally halted.

"Thank you." Ms Carmichael glanced up at the gallery. "You can go now, girls. I don't want to be responsible for making you late for study hall."

Dylan figured that her aunt didn't want to give Honey and Lani her decision with bystanders in the gallery. She hoped that didn't mean there would be bad news. It would be so much fun if Honey and Lani made intermediate.

"Well," Lynsey said as they began to head down the stairs. "I don't think Lani's got much chance of getting into the intermediate programme. If she can't even transition from a trot to a walk, how's she going to jump?"

"Maybe they'll draw up a new programme just for her." Patience let out a low laugh. "I have a feeling lassoing would be her thing."

Dylan felt a surge of annoyance. Just because Lani didn't wear breeches and high boots, that didn't make her any less of a rider! "If you ask me, she deserves to get in just from the way she handled Skylark," she said hotly.

"That whole thing where she crossed her reins was pretty cool. I've never seen that before," Malory agreed. "And she has to have strong legs."

"That's what they teach them at the rodeo," Patience claimed.

Lynsey raised her eyes heavenward. "If she gets into the intermediate programme, I'll eat my jodhpurs."

I'll remember that, Dylan thought, as Patience clutched Lynsey's arm, shaking with laughter.

The seventh grade had Ms Marshall, the other Adams housemother, supervising them for study hall. Even though it was the first day of the semester and the girls didn't have any homework other than to learn some Spanish verbs, she insisted that, instead of getting out early, they had to read one of their assigned books for English literature. The minutes started to drag long before the bell rang.

Dylan stuffed her books into her bag and caught up with Honey and Lani, who were heading down the hallway with Malory. "Hey, you guys, wait up!" she called. "So, how did your assessment go? Did Al— " She caught herself just in time. "Did Ms Carmichael let you know if you made it into the programme?"

"She sure did," Lani grinned. "Honey, do you want to tell Dylan?"

"No, I think you should do it," Honey said.

"But you'd do it so much better than me," Lani replied, straight-faced.

Dylan raised her eyebrows at Malory. But Malory just looked up at the ceiling and began whistling under her breath.

"Aargh! All right, enough already!" Dylan shook a fist in the air.

"We both got in," Honey announced, her brown eyes shining. "She even told Lani that she handled Skylark well, that she's always high-strung after she jumps."

"Way to go!" Dylan exclaimed, giving them both a high five.

"Yeah, things really fell apart after you guys showed up. I'm lucky. Ms Carmichael gave me a break."

"Come on, you deserve it. Dylan and I knew you'd make intermediate," Malory said as they continued walking down the hallway to the cafeteria. "Now we'll all be riding together. I'm so glad Lynsey was wrong."

Dylan stopped as a thought occurred to her. "I've got to go up to my room for something. I'll see you all in the cafeteria." Before the others had a chance to say anything, she turned and hurried back to the stairs, holding back laughter as she devised her plan.

Dylan quickly chose salmon and new potatoes from the serving counter in the cafeteria before joining the other seventh-graders. Honey had saved her a place. As Dylan sat down, she glanced over at Lynsey. "I guess you've heard the great news about Honey and Lani," she enthused.

Lynsey refused to meet her eyes and instead rolled a cherry tomato around her plate with her fork.

"Aren't you hungry?" Dylan asked sympathetically. "Or maybe you're just saving room?"

"For what?" Caught off guard, Lynsey looked up at Dylan.

"Your jodhpurs," Dylan grinned. She pulled a pair of breeches from her shoulder bag, flapping them in the air before placing them on the spare tray she'd brought over. She pushed it across to Lynsey. "Do you want ketchup with that?"

Lynsey glared at Dylan, her blue-grey eyes smoldering. "Whatever." She scowled and shook her head at Dylan, as if she thought her roommate should know better.

"You did say you'd eat your jodhpurs…" Dylan reminded her impishly.

Lani leaned across and prodded the trousers. "Lynsey, I'm concerned that you might have an eating disorder."

Lynsey snatched up the jodhpurs and rolled them in a ball. "Very funny, Dylan. I owe you one," she responded sweetly before turning to Patience. "Did you get a chance to look at the bulletin board and see which movie we're getting tonight?"

"It's *Hidalgo*," Patience replied. "The Viggo Mortensen movie about the Pony Express rider who enters a race across the desert."

"Viggo who?" Lani looked blank.

"Um, Viggo Mortensen," Lynsey said, speaking slowly. "You know, as in the very cute guy from *Lord of the Rings*?"

"*Lord of the Rings* meets the Pony Express. The good folks in Hollywood are really struggling for original ideas, aren't they?" Lani said dryly.

Lynsey shrugged. "I've already seen it. My dad got it for our home movie theatre, but I guess I could see it again."

"Oh, the cinematography is supposed to be great.

73

I've been meaning to see it for a while," Wei Lin said, breaking off from chatting with Razina and Alexandra.

"You can sit with me and I'll explain the difficult parts," Dylan teased Lani as she squeezed some lemon juice over her fish.

"Or if you want to skip it, then you could come down to the stables with me," Malory chipped in. "I asked Ms Carmichael if I could clean some tack or scrub buckets to earn some points for stable management before we get too busy with classes."

"That sounds more like it," said Lani with a grin. "I'm not in the mood to sit around tonight – too much pent-up energy."

Malory glanced across at Dylan. "You don't mind if Lani doesn't watch the movie with you guys, do you?"

Dylan blinked. "No, of course not," she replied, but she couldn't help feeling that Malory had intentionally given Lani a counter-offer. She told herself she was being over-sensitive. It wasn't like she was going to be watching this movie on her own, and, as much as she liked stable work, she felt she had earned a night on the couch.

Dylan squeezed in on the sofa between Razina and Wei Lin. "So," Wei Lin smiled, offering Dylan some popcorn out of the enormous bowl they were sharing. "Does the fact that I'm not into horses mean that I'm not going to understand one word of this movie?"

"No. You can enjoy all of the other parts," Dylan said, throwing a piece of popcorn into the air and catching it in her mouth.

74

"Great," Wei Lin replied, snuggling farther back into the cushions.

"Like Viggo Mortensen all hot and sweaty and smelling like horses!" Dylan added, shouting with laughter as Wei Lin pelted her with one of the plaid throw pillows.

Tanisha Appleton walked over to dim the light before switching on the wide-screen plasma TV and clicking on the DVD remote.

Dylan took another handful of popcorn and handed the bucket to Honey, who was sitting at the end of the sofa. She caught her eye and smiled. So far, boarding school was like one giant sleepover – with the extra bonus of riding!

Chapter Six

Dylan gave the saddle one final rub and admired the soft chestnut glow on the leather. She had passed up the opportunity to go on a shopping trip to the mall in Cheney Falls. It had been such a busy first week that she much preferred the idea of chilling out in the stable.

"Do you want a hand with that?" she asked Honey, who was wrestling with Hardy's bridle after taking it apart for a thorough cleaning.

"I'm fine, thanks," said Honey, without looking up from buckling one of the cheekpieces.

Dylan looked over at Lani and Malory, who were soaping saddles on the other side of the tack room. They had already been hard at work when Dylan arrived. Then Honey had joined them half an hour later, after writing a postcard to her brother. Dylan had the sneaking suspicion that they were all there for the same reason: they hoped they might be told they could ride, even though it was the weekend. Usually, weekend sessions were purely make-up or were scheduled in advance for a student needing help in a particular discipline. The Adams girls hoped cleaning tack would earn them points with the stable staff. "I'm going to get a soda, can I get you guys anything?" offered Dylan.

"I'd take her up on her offer – she doesn't make them that often," a voice said from the doorway.

Dylan spun around. "Nat!"

Her cousin held up his hand for a high five. His amber eyes twinkled as he dodged to avoid Dylan ruffling his fox-coloured hair – it wasn't that hard, since he was at least eight inches taller than she was. "So you've survived your first week?" he teased. "I'll admit, I'm impressed."

"You should be." Dylan smiled. She turned back to the other girls, who were staring at Nat with open curiosity. "Guys, this is my cousin, Nat. He's a freshman at Saint Kit's. You know, the boys' school on the other side of Cheney Falls? The dark side."

"Just so you know, the bad sense of humour does not run in the family," Nat said solemnly. "How are you all doing?"

"You know, you sort of remind me of someone – and it's not Dylan," Lani said, squinting her eyes and screwing up her mouth as she took in Nat's high cheekbones.

"That would be my mom," he told her.

"How on earth would she know your mom?" Honey asked, dropping her sponge into the bucket at her feet.

"Um, Nat's mom is Ms Carmichael," Dylan told

them, feeling uncomfortable. "As in, Ali Carmichael." Dylan hadn't told anyone that she was related to the riding director, but now she was kind of glad it was out in the open.

"Oh." Lani paused for a minute. "She's your aunt? I guess that's pretty cool."

"That explains how you knew that paint pony!" Honey exclaimed, putting it all together. "You're so lucky. I'd love it if someone in my family was into horses. Whenever I started talking about Rocky back home, everyone's eyes sort of glazed over."

"Yeah," Malory said quietly. "She'd be a cool aunt."

"Do you know where she is?" Nat asked, glancing at Dylan. "Maybe you could show me around?"

"Sure. See you later, guys," Dylan said, following Nat out of the tack room.

"I think Ms Carmichael is schooling Quince," Dylan said, leading the way out of the barn and onto the yard.

"It sounds so weird hearing you call her that," Nat said, sticking his hands in his jeans and kicking at a small stone. He glanced at Dylan, narrowing his eyes. "I hope I didn't make things tricky for you back there. I'd have thought by now your friends would know that you're her niece."

Dylan shrugged. "I didn't want anyone thinking that I was going to be getting any special treatment. I mean, your mom will be selecting the competition teams. I really want to make it, but only if I deserve it."

"Don't you think your friends would understand that?"

"Well, it takes a little bit to know who your friends are – who you want to tell, you know," Dylan tried to explain.

"That makes sense," Nat agreed. "They all seemed really nice back there. I'm sure your secret's safe."

"Oh, I don't really care anymore. I'm actually relieved you blew my cover."

"Anytime, Dyl." Nat gave her a playful jab in the shoulder.

They came to the outdoor ring and leaned on the gate to watch Ali riding. Quince was working at an extended trot across the ring, and Dylan thought the dappled grey mare looked fantastic, with her neck arched and her long silver tail streaming in the air like a banner. Quince was her aunt's competition horse, a Thoroughbred with an unpredictable stable temperament but outstanding manners in the ring.

"Hey, Mom!" Nat put his fingers in his mouth and let out a piercing whistle.

Ali looked their way and, seeing who it was, stood up in her stirrups and pushed Quince into a canter while she held the reins in one hand and waved with the other. Dylan grinned – this was the Aunt Ali she knew, goofing around, instead of Ms Carmichael, Director of Riding.

It always amazed her that Ali was actually her mom's sister – she seemed to have more in common with Dylan's laid-back, horse-loving dad.

Ali pulled Quince to a stop and slid off, laughing as she hugged Nat across the gate. "You're early," she said as Dylan took Quince's reins, reaching up to scratch the mare's damp neck.

"Good to see you, too, Mom," Nat said. "I'll just come back next week."

"Don't you dare!" Ali said quickly. "I just need five minutes to cool Quince off and then I'll be ready. Dylan can take you up to my office, and I'll catch up as soon as I'm done, OK?"

"Sure," Nat said.

"Thanks, Dylan," Ali said, retaking the reins. "Nat and I are going to grab a bite to eat in town before I drop him back at Saint Kit's. Do you want to come with us?"

"That would be great," Dylan said.

"So you like snails, right?" Nat said, as they turned to walk back up the path. "We're going to this French restaurant, and if you don't eat the complimentary snails they serve as appetizers, the maître d' gets really offended."

Nat was always playing pranks on her, and Dylan wasn't going to get suckered again. "Sure, I like snails," she said, straight-faced. "Especially the small ones – they're extra slimy – a lot like warm snot."

"Gross!" Nat's face wrinkled. "I swear you should have been a boy."

"I swear you should have been one, too," Dylan snapped back.

It was a long-standing joke between them that Dylan wasn't a typical girl – not in the demure, polished ways her mom would like her to be. She had her dad's sense of humour and his athleticism. Dylan was more like her mom's sister, Aunt Ali, than she was like her mother. And Nat was the perfect stand-in big brother for Dylan, who was an only child.

"You'd do anything for a laugh," Nat said.

"It runs in the family" Dylan laughed as she reached for the doorknob of her aunt's office. Just then, a blue roan trotted past and clattered onto the yard.

Lynsey circled Bluegrass back toward them.

Lynsey certainly hasn't mastered the art of subtlety, Dylan thought, watching how her roommate swiftly assessed her cousin.

"Slipping into the director's office with an unannounced visitor, Dylan?" Lynsey questioned in a conspiratorial tone. "Well, this certainly improves my opinion of you."

"Don't let it," Dylan quickly announced. "He's my cousin."

"Oh, well." Lynsey pulled off her hat and ran her fingers through her hair, giving Nat a wide smile. "I'm Lynsey Harrison. I room with Dylan."

"I'm Nat Carmichael. My mom works here."

This news caused Lynsey to pause, but to Dylan's amazement, Lynsey didn't comment on the connection. She did, however, drop her riding crop.

"Oops," she said, looking at Nat and making no effort to pick it up.

You've gotta be kidding me, a voice in Dylan's head groaned, as Nat bent down to retrieve the crop. *Someone should just hit her with that thing. Knock some sense into her.*

"Ms Carmichael is going to meet us here," Dylan

said in a warning tone. "I'll come back in about fifteen minutes," she added, not wanting to hang around to see any more of Lynsey's overt flirtations. If Nat fell for Lynsey's fake 'n' bake charms, Dylan was going to be seriously disappointed in him.

Dylan decided to go to the student centre to grab a bottled water and send some emails to her friends back home before meeting Ali and Nat for their lunch date.

"Hey, Dylan. Wait up!" She turned to see Malory jogging across the yard. "I told Kelly and Sarah I'd help with the mucking out. Do you want to pitch in?"

Dylan started to wonder if Malory spent any time away from the stables. "I was just going to send some emails home before going out for lunch," she explained. "Any other time, and I'd be there."

"Are you going anywhere nice?" Malory asked.

"Some French restaurant," Dylan told her.

"*Très mal*," Malory said.

Dylan glanced at her. "Um, I think you mean *très bon*."

"Why, what did I say?" Malory pushed her hair off her forehead.

"'Very bad!'" Dylan grinned. "Although if I have to eat snails like Nat is threatening, you may not be too far off the mark."

"I guess I need to spend more time with my French book. I think there's a quiz next week." Malory looked a little bewildered. "Well, I'll see you later, then," she said, turning to head down the path that led to the barn.

But Dylan was only half paying attention. She was peering over Malory's shoulder at the pony being ridden a short distance away in the outdoor arena.

"I'm sure that's Morello." She frowned. She hadn't been able to ride Morello yet, so she was surprised to see him being worked on a weekend.

Malory looked toward the ring, shading her eyes. "Shouldn't there be a trainer somewhere?" she asked in surprise.

"That's exactly what I was thinking," Dylan agreed. Students were forbidden to ride unsupervised in the arenas, especially if they were jumping.

They could see Morello trotting down the far side of the ring. As he reached the corner, his rider gave him a kick, which made him trot faster. The rider then shook the reins and kicked harder, driving him into a rocky canter. Morello swerved off the rail, and Dylan gasped. "She's going to jump him!" she yelled. There was a fence about halfway up the ring, nearly three feet in height. Without saying another word, Dylan and Malory hurried to the arena.

He looks crooked, Dylan thought. Even from a distance, she could tell that Morello was not straight. She held her breath, and at the last minute, the pony veered away from the jump. Thrown onto Morello's neck, the rider had to grab his mane to keep from falling off.

They were close enough that Dylan now recognized the rider. It was Emily Page, a seventh-grader from Curie House who was in the basic riding programme.

"Bad boy," Emily shouted, yanking roughly on the reins. Morello pinned his ears and raised his head, shuffling backward several steps and flashing the whites of his eyes. He had broken into a sweat, and when Emily pushed him into a trot, his normally fluid stride was choppy.

"What's she doing?" Malory exclaimed.

"I don't know." Dylan shook her head in horror. Something had to be terribly wrong for Morello to refuse a fence, and she worried what Emily might try next.

As Morello neared where Dylan and Malory were standing, Dylan cupped her hands over her mouth and called, "Where's Ms Phillips?"

"In the office," Emily replied, kicking Morello into a canter again.

"You'd better wait!" Malory shouted, but Emily ignored her and nudged Morello with her heel as he neared the fence.

This time the gelding evened his pace and made a brave try, even though the stride still wasn't right. But he took off too soon and hit the pole with his hind legs. Emily fell onto his neck, and when Morello landed awkwardly on the other side, she turned a somersault right onto the ground. She lay unmoving on the sand, in a small crumpled heap.

"Oh, no!" Malory cried. "She fell off!"

Chapter Seven

Dylan pulled open the gate and sprinted across the sandy arena with Malory right behind her. Morello was standing a few metres away from Emily, his reins trailing on the ground. As the girls came closer, the pony snorted and shied away.

Dylan's chest tightened. She knew if his legs got tangled up in his reins, he could hurt himself. Leaving Malory to see to Emily, she moved slowly toward the paint gelding. "Steady, Morello. Whoa, there's a good boy."

His whole body was tense, and his eyes rolled. He snorted and raised his head, but he didn't move away. Dylan took a step closer and slowly reached out her hand to catch his reins.

"Dylan! Run and get Ms Phillips, now!" Malory's voice rang through the air.

Morello threw up his head, nostrils flaring, and sprang into a trot.

Dylan cursed under her breath. Morello's reins

whipped around his legs, making him more scared as his trot turned into a canter. There was no way she'd be able to catch him now. She had to make sure he didn't get out of the ring.

She turned and raced past Malory, who had helped Emily sit up and was unbuckling her riding hat. "I can't catch Morello," she explained breathlessly. "I need to shut the gate."

"He'll be fine. You need to get Ms Phillips," Malory shouted after her.

Is she crazy? Dylan thought. *Emily's the one who looks fine. If Morello keeps running and steps on his reins, he could fall and break a leg.* She reached the gate and slammed it shut. She spun around to look at Morello, who was careering around the ring. Suddenly he stumbled to a halt. Dylan froze. His foreleg was caught in the reins. Morello's head was lowered, the reins taut between his leg and the bit. Dylan knew that if he panicked he could get into real trouble. All she wanted to do was run over to him and help, but she knew he was nervous and volatile. The last thing she wanted to do was spook him. She looked toward the office, wishing that Ms Phillips would appear around the corner. Emily was sitting up on her own now and talking with Malory, so Dylan made up her mind. She took slow, methodical steps toward Morello, being careful not to startle the pony.

She was so close now she could hear the gelding's noisy breathing. She could see the tension in his neck, where he was straining against the reins. "Whoa, boy. It's OK. I want to help you," she said, trying to keep her voice calm. She reached out and placed a hand on his withers, and his muscles twitched. She gently ran her other hand down his foreleg. "Up," she said, leaning lightly against his shoulder, just as she had done dozens of times to pick his hooves. Morello shifted his weight slightly and carefully lifted his foot. Quickly, Dylan grabbed for the reins and unlooped them from Morello's leg. She straightened up with a sigh and rubbed Morello's forehead.

"Don't ever do that to me again," she told him, feeling wobbly with relief.

She led him back to Malory and Emily. "Everything's under control with Morello." She held out the reins, expecting Malory to take them so she could then get Ms Phillips, but Malory was too focused on Emily. Dylan was surprised to see that Emily looked very pale, even though she was up on her feet. "Are you OK?"

"Where's Ms Phillips?" Malory demanded before Emily could answer.

Dylan frowned. "I already told you. I needed to help Morello first. I'll go get her now."

"No, Dylan. It's too late for that. What if Emily had been seriously hurt? At the worst, Morello would have broken his reins. You need to get your priorities straight," Malory argued.

Dylan's temper flared in response. "My priorities? Look at how stressed he is!" She jerked her head at Morello, whose sides were still heaving. "None of this would have happened if Ms Phillips had been here in the first place." She glared at Emily.

Malory shrugged. "Maybe, but you should quit acting like you're the only one who knows how to handle Morello. It's not like he's yours. He's here for everyone to use, and it's obvious that not everyone is going to ride him the same way as you."

Dylan felt like she'd been slapped across the face. Why was Malory suddenly the moral judge around here? And how did Dylan become the bad guy when Emily was so clearly in the wrong? She took a step back and slowly clapped her hands. "And the smugness trophy goes to Malory O'Neil," she declared, feeling her red-hot temper cool to ice. "It must be such a step down for you to be here at Chestnut Hill, since you clearly think that you are so much better than anyone else."

Malory's cheeks flamed. She stared at Dylan, not saying anything.

"I did what I thought was right," Dylan said plainly.

Malory narrowed her eyes. "I'm taking Emily up to the office. You can take care of Morello. I'm sure you want it that way." She slipped her arm through Emily's and led her in the direction of the gate.

Dylan stared after the two girls for a moment and then turned back to Morello. "Did you get any of that?" she asked, spreading her hands out.

Morello let out a heavy sigh, as if their argument was way beneath him.

"Come on, boy," Dylan said. "Let's get you back to your stable. I've got a lunch date." But the last thing she felt like doing was going out to socialize. All she really wanted to do was curl up in the bed of straw in

Morello's stall and figure out what had just gone wrong between her and Malory. She couldn't remember exactly what she had said to Malory. She had a bad feeling it might be something she would regret, but when she played the scene with Morello and Emily over in her head, she still felt she had made the right decision for Morello.

One thing's for sure, she thought ruefully as she patted Morello. *My priorities seem pretty straight to me.*

Dylan hadn't talked to Malory for the rest of the weekend, and from what she could tell, Malory hadn't told her side of the story to anyone else. So no one knew that something had happened between them, but it was obvious to Dylan. Malory was more reserved than ever around her – and that was saying something. She only seemed comfortable around the stable – or when they were all talking about riding – so it was upsetting for that to be where their problems had started.

For now, however, Dylan was able to focus on something else. It was their first full class with Ali Carmichael as instructor – and she had assigned Dylan to ride Morello. It was her first time on him since arriving at Chestnut Hill, and he was just as wonderful as she had remembered.

As they started on the course Ali had set for their lesson, she could hardly stop the big grin that spread across her face. But the grin faded as they came around the turn to the double. This was a serious fence!

Dylan slowed Morello's stride by straightening in the saddle and closing her fingers on the reins. *One, two, three*, she counted, then bent forward from the waist for the take-off. Morello sprang neatly over the first jump and put in two short strides to sail over the second. He thudded down on the other side and gave a playful buck.

"Good boy!" Dylan exclaimed as she trotted him to the other end of the jumping arena, patting him on the neck the whole way. She had been the last to jump in their lesson, and the ground had been a little torn up in places, but Morello had been a star. Dylan was relieved that the events of last Saturday hadn't seemed to affect him at all. He hadn't shown any reluctance or wariness after the Emily episode. She slowed the paint gelding to a walk as they drew nearer the rest of the class. There were thirteen intermediate riders in seventh grade, split into two classes. Today, both groups were practicing their jumping – Dylan was in her aunt's group, in the outdoor arena, while Ms Phillips was working with her class indoors.

"Way to go," Lynsey said when Dylan halted alongside Bluegrass. "That was a great round, even if you did knock the wall."

Dylan looked at her in surprise. "Thanks!" she said. "It was all Morello. He saved me at the wall. I turned way too sharply. If I hadn't done that, we might have gotten a clear round." The fences at Chestnut Hill were far more sensitive than those at Dylan's old stable. It didn't take much to drop a pole or knock over some other element of a fence. Still, it seemed Lynsey managed a clean round almost every time.

"Oh, don't worry about a little thing like that," Lynsey said generously, and for a moment Dylan wondered if she needed to rethink her opinion of her roommate. "You're sure to make the junior jumping team with a performance like that. And with your aunt being the Director of Riding, I guess it wouldn't matter if you'd knocked down a few more." She gazed innocently at Dylan, giving her a bright smile.

"Everyone form a line, please," Ali Carmichael called before Dylan could come up with an appropriately biting response.

Still fuming, Dylan reined Morello back a few steps so Lani could turn Colorado and drop into the line.

"I wouldn't take any notice of our friend over there," Lani said in a low voice. "She's just mad because you rode the course better than she did – and on an inferior animal!" She delivered the last few words in a perfect mimic of Lynsey and then grinned. Her smile was so bright and wide, Dylan wasn't sure if she was still mocking Lynsey. Regardless, Lani always seemed to make Dylan feel better.

Dylan noticed Malory walking Hardy farther down the row as they lined up, and Dylan realized she was deliberately putting Lani and Honey between them. Dylan was beginning to see that Malory was every bit as stubborn as she was, and she wondered if their disagreement would come to an easy resolution.

"You all did great today. I'm seeing some real

improvement. If I didn't know better, I'd swear you were trying to impress me!" Ali said, standing in front of the group.

The girls exchanged glances and slightly nervous smiles. It wasn't a secret that they all had the team tryouts on their minds. The trainers would select the junior jumping team in just a few weeks, and competition was already fierce.

Ali Carmichael looked at Dylan. "That was a solid round. It was a shame you tipped the wall – next time watch Morello's stride more carefully as he comes out of the corner." Dylan nodded, knowing that tight corners were one of her weak spots, especially when she was trying to maintain a faster pace.

"I know you've all tried a selection of ponies since you arrived," Ali continued, looking at each girl in turn. "We wanted to find the mount that best matches your individual strengths and style."

This is it! Dylan thought, certain that Ali was about to announce which ponies they would ride for tryouts. She crossed her fingers.

Ms Carmichael hesitated. "I think the best thing is if you stick with the ponies you're riding now. I'm happy with the pairings from today, and since the tryouts are a few weeks away, you should have ample time to build a good bond. I wish you all the best luck."

Things were starting to look much brighter! Dylan was tempted to let out a whoop of joy at the thought of riding Morello exclusively for the next few weeks. Riding Morello would give her the best chance to make the team. It had been months since they last jumped a course together, and they were still totally in sync. She leaned forward to rub his neck and noticed Malory, farther down the line on Hardy, doing the same. In spite of their argument, Dylan was glad Malory was pleased with Ali's choice of pony for her.

"The team consists of four regular riders plus a reserve," Ali Carmichael told them. "And since you'll be up against the rest of the seventh *and* eighth grade, competition is going to be pretty tough. Most ponies will have two riders, and we'll draw names to see which rider goes first."

"I don't have to share Bluegrass, do I?" Lynsey protested.

Ms Carmichael started to shake her head.

"That's just as well – he's very sensitive, and I doubt he'd go well for anyone else," Lynsey added before Ali could say anything.

"Well, if he's as sensitive as you say, maybe you should think about using one of the Chestnut Hill ponies," Ali returned evenly. "Keep in mind, if you make the team, your mount becomes part of the team. There are circumstances when others – sometimes even riders from other schools – would be required to ride your horse."

Dylan hid her smile behind her gloved hand. She couldn't imagine Lynsey being at all happy about someone else riding Bluegrass. Nor could she picture Lynsey astride a common school pony, but Dylan knew there was nothing common about Morello. *It's time to get serious*, she told herself. *You have three weeks to get good enough on Morello to make the team. Don't screw it up.*

"Dylan!" Lani's voice called through the door. "If you don't come out right now, I'm gonna come in and drag you out by your hair!"

Dylan grinned and quickly finished running a tube of Gash lip gloss over her bottom lip. She tiptoed over to the door and yanked it open. Still holding onto the knob, Lani staggered into the room.

"Would you hurry up? I've been waiting for you forever," Dylan scolded, straight-faced. "It's not like I have a date with fifty boys every night of the week."

"Whatever, Walsh," Lani retorted. She picked up Dylan's comb and ran it through her hair. "Honey and I have already divided them between us."

There was an evening discussion for the riding students scheduled in the school auditorium, but the fact that the boys from Saint Kit's would be there had generated more excitement than the symposium itself.

"You guys, come on!" called Honey.

"After you." Dylan waved her arm at the door.

"No, after you, I insist," Lani grinned. "You're going to need all the help you can get tonight. But I doubt that a head start will do you much good."

"Hey!" Honey popped her head through the door, her blond hair worked neatly into a French braid. "If we don't leave right now, we'll get locked out of the auditorium altogether, and then we'll see how many dates you get."

Dylan and Lani looked at each other and burst into laughter, each taking Honey by an arm as they escorted her down the hall.

The campus was lit with yellow light spilling from Victorian lampposts. Dylan, Lani, and Honey hurried along the path to the auditorium, hoping they wouldn't be the last to arrive. The talk was on alternative treatments for horses, and Dylan was really looking forward to hearing Amy Fleming, one of the scheduled speakers.

"I remember reading an article about her," she said as they headed up the steps that led into the arts building. "She worked at this place called Heartland, and she practically ran it by the time she was sixteen. Can you imagine that?"

The others didn't answer, and when Dylan glanced up she saw why. On the top step stood Ms Marshall, the Adams House high-school housemother, and she glared down at the tardy students as she held open the main door.

"You're late," she said, walking ahead of them down a hallway and pushing open another set of doors. "There are some seats on the left with the rest of the seventh grade. Please sit there," she whispered, nodding into the darkened auditorium.

As the girls tiptoed down the dimly lit aisle, they could hear Dr Starling introducing the first speaker, Dr Jeremy Haslum, who was a professor of veterinary studies at Virginia Tech.

"Sorry," Dylan whispered as she stepped on Grace

Findlay's toe. The eighth-grade intermediate rider stood up to let Lani and Honey pass, clearly not trusting them to find their way to the spare seats without crushing her feet as well.

They pulled down their theatre seats, and Dylan realized that she was sitting next to Malory. Malory stared straight ahead at Dr Haslum, who was pointing to a diagram of a horse. Dylan wondered if Malory was ignoring her or just concentrating on the speaker. She wished she hadn't lashed out against her classmate, yet she wasn't sure how to take it back. Her words had no doubt been hurtful, even if they were just said in the heat of the moment.

Dylan peered at the right-hand side of the auditorium, where the Saint Kit's boys were sitting. Although the lights were dimmed, she could just make out their profiles.

"You're supposed to be here for the talk, not to ogle boys," Lani muttered out of the side of her mouth.

"Ditto," Dylan whispered behind her hand, noticing that Lani's head was also swiveled to the right.

There was a cute dark-haired boy in the third row who kept glancing in their direction. Dylan nudged Lani, but the boy must have seen her, because he quickly looked back at the stage and didn't turn around again.

"Who do you think he was checking out?" Dylan whispered.

"If you ask me, it was Mal," Lani muttered. She leaned across Dylan to ask, "Hey, did you see your secret admirer?"

Malory was silent for a moment. Then, when Dr Haslum paused to move on to the next slide, she whispered back, "His name is Caleb Smith. I met him in the summer. He was riding at my stable."

"So he's your boyfriend?" Lani asked in a loud hiss, causing girls from the row in front to turn around.

"No!" Malory protested, still facing the stage. "He's just a friend."

Lynsey was sitting in the row behind them, with Patience, Razina, and a girl from Curie. She leaned forward. "Who did you say that guy is? Patience wants to know."

"Lynsey!" Patience gasped.

"Shh!" The warning had come from the upperclassmen's section, and the younger students quickly quieted down.

Dylan settled back into her seat and listened to the end of the doctor's lecture on conventional veterinary medicine. Dylan found just about any equine discussion interesting, but it was the next speaker she was really waiting for.

"I'm going to hand you over for the rest of evening to Amy Fleming," the professor announced at last. "She's not only a successful equine therapist, she also happens to be one of my students." He put down his laser pen and smiled at the slim girl with long, light-brown hair who stood up to join him.

"I wonder who her stylist is?" Dylan overheard Lynsey whisper. Amy's simple trouser suit fit her well but was clearly not from a Lynsey-approved boutique.

As far as Dylan could tell, the only makeup she was wearing was mascara. She didn't really need any more. The young equine therapist had a very natural beauty that didn't require flashy clothes or two-tone eyeshadow. Amy Fleming obviously had more important things to think about.

"Hi." Amy spoke in a clear, pleasant voice. "I've been asked here tonight to tell you a little about the work that I've done to help horses, using complementary methods." She looked around the auditorium, her grey eyes glowing with enthusiasm and possibly a little apprehension.

She couldn't be any older than eighteen, Dylan realized, surprised that anyone that age could have enough experience to be speaking in a lecture.

"Complementary methods are also known as alternative therapies," Amy continued. "These are ways to treat a horse in addition to traditional medicine." She pushed a button, and a diagram filled the screen behind her. She explained that it showed various pressure points on a horse's body. "T-touch – a circular massaging movement – has been proven to increase relaxation of horses and other animals when pressure is applied to these areas. A horse doesn't even need to be sick to benefit from this procedure.

"My mother spent many years experimenting with various herbal treatments, especially Bach Flower Remedies," Amy went on. She glanced down at the floor for a moment. "She had this amazing notebook that detailed what each flower could do. I can't tell you how many horses that notebook helped save," she continued. Hearing a catch in her voice, Dylan remembered from the article she'd read that Amy's mom had died several years ago, leaving Amy to carry on her work alone. Dylan felt a tug of sympathy.

"Next, I'm going to show a short film about the join up – a technique we use at Heartland for gaining horses' trust," Amy said, picking up the remote control.

A long-legged, dark roan colt flickered up on the screen above the stage, trotting around an outdoor arena. "This is Spindleberry," Amy explained. Her voice softened, and Dylan wondered if she herself sounded so totally smitten with Morello when she talked about him. "He's being trained using all of the techniques I'm telling you about this evening. He arrived at Heartland extremely dehydrated. If we hadn't rescued him, he might have died. We used conventional and complementary methods to save him, and then we started emotional therapy. One of the ways we gained his trust was by using join up." The screen showed Amy standing in the middle of the arena, flicking a lead rope at the colt, to send him cantering around in circles.

Dylan frowned. *How could that encourage the colt to put his trust in anyone? It looks like she's just chasing him away.*

As if she'd read Dylan's thoughts, Amy went on to explain, "It might seem strange that I'm chasing him away from me, but it's the first stage to winning his complete trust. I keep driving him away until he acknowledges that I would make a great herd leader and what he actually wants is to depend on me for protection – for survival, even. This appeals to a horse's herding instincts." Moments later the camera showed the colt lowering his head, and then he started opening and closing his mouth as if he were trying to chew air.

"This is it," Amy said quietly. "This is his way of saying that he doesn't want to run from me anymore and that he trusts me to look after him because I'm tougher than he is. It's very interesting. All horses convey this with the same signs – the lowered head and the chewing."

Dylan sat forward on the edge of her chair. She didn't take her eyes off the colt as he slowed to a trot. His hooves brushed over the sandy surface, while his inside ear flickered toward the girl in the centre of the ring.

"Watch what happens when I turn my back on him," Amy urged.

Hardly breathing, Dylan watched as Spindleberry turned into the centre of the ring and walked up to Amy, eventually nudging her back with his nose. A spontaneous round of applause went up as the screen showed Amy walking forward, the colt matching her stride for stride as if they were attached with an invisible thread. "By deciding for himself not to keep running away from me, he's formed a bond between the two of us. That bond is based on mutual respect and trust – something that a whip and spurs can never bring." Amy turned back around to face everyone. "Any questions?" she asked when the lights were turned back on. She grinned, suddenly looking very young, and a sea of hands appeared all over the auditorium.

The questions ran overtime, and when Amy was finally allowed to sit down, the auditorium erupted with more applause. Dylan stood up, clapping hard, wondering if any of the Heartland methods would be incorporated into their own riding programmes.

Lani put her fingers into her mouth and let out a piercing wolf whistle as the Saint Kit's teachers began moving down the aisle to escort the boys back to their bus. Dylan caught sight of Nat as he was leaving the auditorium, and he waved to her, then shrugged to show that he couldn't stay to talk. She wondered briefly why he'd bothered coming to the symposium – after all, he wasn't interested in horses, in spite of growing up around them all his life. *He must have come to give Aunt Ali some moral support for her first interschool event*, she guessed.

"I wish I'd had a chance to say hi to Nat," Lynsey commented as the girls walked back to the dorm. She looked at Dylan. "How can he afford to go to somewhere like Saint Kit's? I mean, his mom's just a riding instructor."

Dylan felt a slow anger begin to swirl inside her. She was sure there was a tuition-support arrangement between Saint Kit's and Chestnut Hill staff members, but she wasn't about to explain that to Lynsey. Instead she turned to Lani and stated in a loud voice, "Hey, did

I tell you about Nat's dad? He's a big-time graphic designer. He just won some award for his work with Diamond Spring."

"Wow – I know that brand. It's like sparkling water and fruit juice, right? It looks like high-end stuff," Lani said, matching Dylan's forced tone but still sounding impressed.

"Oh, it is. They had it at my club," Lynsey said, as if Dylan had been including her all along. "Well, now that I know a little more about him, I can go ahead and get him to ask me out."

Now that you have a better sense of his financial pedigree, you mean, Dylan thought, furious. She glanced over at Malory, who seemed unfazed by the conversation. She had been quiet since identifying the curly-headed boy at the convocation.

"If that girl with all her *alternative* ideas hadn't run overtime, I'd have gotten a chance to talk to him tonight," Lynsey added, emphasizing alternative with air quotes.

Dylan was just about to defend Amy Fleming's methods, since they clearly got results, when Malory jumped in. Her blue eyes were shining, and there was a spot of colour on both her cheeks, as if she'd been outside in the wind. "I think it was a great talk, and I wouldn't mind trying some of her techniques myself. Better to treat a horse with respect and understanding than to try and control him with a whip and fear. I'd rather work *with* a horse than *against* one."

"Absolutely. I know I'm still learning about horses, but her approach convinced me," Razina agreed.

Malory's unexpected outburst managed to silence even Lynsey. *I just never know which way that girl is going to jump*, Dylan thought in surprise.

Chapter Eight

Dylan was determined to work her heart and soul out. Whatever it took to get on that team with Morello, she was willing to do it. An extra practice session had been scheduled on Friday after morning classes, and she was thrilled with how well things were going – she and Morello seemed to share the same rhythm. Ali had set up a practice jump in one half of the arena for those waiting to take the course of jumps in the other half. Not only had Morello cleared the practice jump with a foot and a half to spare, he was now flying around the main course.

Dylan slowed Morello to steady him for the fence that every other rider except Malory had knocked down. "Take it easy, boy," she murmured, feeling him pull against her hands. Obediently, Morello slowed, and Dylan held him together as they rounded the corner. The fence was a tall upright that was particularly nasty since it was the first jump out of a fast turn. Morello cleared the gate without even rattling it.

"Good boy!" Dylan whispered. She turned him in a circle toward the parallel bars that marked the halfway point of the course. There was no way she wasn't going clear now!

"That's enough, Dylan. Bring him in, please." Ali Carmichael's voice rang across the yard before Dylan reached the next fence.

Dylan reined Morello in, staring at her aunt in confusion. She hadn't stopped any of the other girls partway through the twelve-fence course. "But I haven't finished," she argued.

"Now, please, Dylan. Morello's had enough." Her aunt's tone was clipped.

Shaking her head, but not daring to say any more, Dylan rode Morello out of the ring. Her face felt hot as she wondered whether Ali would have let another rider finish the round. She caught sight of Lynsey's smug expression and tried not to scowl.

I don't know why I was concerned that people would think I'd get special treatment because I'm the riding director's niece. If anything, it's the other way around!

"Hey, Dylan. Wait up!"

Dylan turned to see Honey and Lynsey hurrying down the hallway after her. She was on her way to study hall and had so far managed to avoid them since the riding session. She wasn't feeling up to any of Lynsey's wisecracks about the way Ali had stopped her halfway around the course.

"Seems like your disappearing back is all we've

seen of you today," Lynsey declared as they caught up with her.

"Obviously I need to perfect my technique a little more," Dylan said pointedly.

"I'm sure Ms Carmichael wasn't singling you out," Honey said.

"She didn't stop anybody else before they completed the course," Dylan grumbled. "She said 'Morello's had enough.' What does that mean?"

"Maybe Morello's fitness level isn't as high as the other horses," Honey suggested.

"After all, this is his first year at Chestnut Hill." Lynsey smiled, twisting Honey's well-meant comment. "Maybe he's not up to intermediate-level workouts."

Dylan stared at her, deciding whether she'd give Lynsey the satisfaction of acknowledging her insult. Lynsey knew full well that Morello had tons of talent and had gone well in all the previous intermediate classes.

Ignoring her, Dylan stalked across the half-full classroom. The desks were set out in rows so students could work without being distracted. She glanced over to see who was monitoring them for the study period. Everyone dreaded having Ms Marshall, because she came ready and willing to distribute extra work if anyone finished her assignments early. Dylan breathed a sigh of relief when she saw Mrs Hudson's red hair bent over a book at the front desk. The art teacher usually became so engrossed with sketching in her pad that she didn't notice what the girls were doing, as long as they kept quiet.

Dylan headed for her favorite desk. It was close to the window and had a fabulous view of the campus. This afternoon there was hardly anyone outside except for Mr Lyttle, one of the grounds assistants. He was busy raking up grass clippings and stacking the bags in the wagon attached to the back of his riding mower. Dylan sat down and began to pull out her books. *I'm never going to be able to concentrate on studying*, she thought. The demise of the riding lesson was in the centre of her brain, and it wasn't going anywhere anytime soon. Her round had been going so well that she couldn't figure out why her aunt had stopped her short.

Dylan wasn't the only one who was restless; none of the girls seemed able to settle into their homework if the paper shuffling, coughs, and sighs were anything to go by.

Dylan stared at the page in her geography book and realized she had read the same paragraph on irrigation three times. She leaned back and stretched her arms above her head. She frowned as she saw Patience pass a note to Razina and then nod her head in Dylan's direction. *What's up?* Dylan wondered. *Something fun, please. It feels like I haven't laughed in forever.*

Razina spent a few seconds reading the note and then glanced up at Mrs Hudson. The art teacher was hard at work with her charcoal pencil, so Razina held her arm out for Dylan to take the piece of paper. Dylan quickly leaned over her desk and grabbed the note. She smoothed out the paper and read: *All Adams seventh-*

grade girls are invited to a truth-or-dare game tonight at 11pm in Room Three. Be there, or be you know what!

Dylan felt excitement shoot up her spine. She loved truth-or-dare! When they'd played it at camp last summer, she'd out-dared everyone by swimming across the lake and hanging their counsellor's swim trunks from a tree on the other side. She was totally up for this. Folding up the note, she tossed it over her shoulder to Lani, who let out an exclamation that made everyone in the room look her way. Dylan glanced over her shoulder and saw Lani rubbing her forehead. Dylan raised her eyebrows and looked pointedly at the note teetering on the edge of Lani's desk. Lani snaked out her hand to catch the paper.

"Is everything OK, Lani?" Mrs Hudson asked, looking up.

"Yes, Mrs Hudson. I ... I almost dropped my book," Lani said as she pushed the note up her sleeve, her brown eyes full of innocence.

Dylan grinned and turned back in her seat as Mrs Hudson walked up their row, running her eyes over each of their books.

"Well, from what I can see, there's not a whole lot of work going on here," the teacher said, standing over Dylan's desk and looking down at the snowy white page of her notebook. "You had better get a move on unless you want to be eating dinner at your desks tonight."

Dylan picked up her pen and tried to look as if she was hard at work, but now her mind was filled with thoughts of the night ahead. How come she could devise a truth and a dare for every girl on the floor, but she couldn't focus enough to answer the first question on her geography handout? *Who cares?* she thought. *It's almost the weekend, and truth-or-dare is less than six hours away.*

Lights were out at ten and the girls had to lie in the dark for the next hour, until they were certain the housemothers were fast asleep. Dylan had set her cell phone to vibrate at ten fifty-five in case she snoozed, but everyone in her room was too excited to slumber. They took turns talking about life at home and what they'd done that summer, and when Dylan pressed the "off" button on her phone, she figured there wasn't a lot more truth about themselves that they could reveal for the game. Now it officially felt like they were roommates. Even Lynsey seemed to have let down her guard – Dylan was almost considering the possibility that the majority of Lynsey's wicked, mocking, egotistic attitude was an act. *No one is that conceited*, Dylan insisted to herself. *But not even that semi-revelation would alter Dylan's take-no-prisoners game plan for truth-or-dare.*

She kicked off her covers and stood up, her heart racing with the knowledge that they were going against house rules.

"Ready?" Honey whispered, clicking on her flashlight and accidentally shining it straight in Dylan's eyes. "Oh, sorry."

Dylan pretended to faint, and Honey gave an explosive laugh.

"Shhh, you guys. You're gonna get us caught!" Lynsey hissed.

Dylan reached under her bed to get the plate of cupcakes she had commandeered from the student centre. She slid her feet into her blue sheepskin slippers and padded to the door, holding it open for the others to slip out. Then, suppressing nervous laughter all the way, she followed Honey's flashlight down the hall.

The rest of the girls were already waiting inside Patience's room. A faint eerie light shone from a bedside lamp that had been put down on the floor, and there was a pile of food on a coffee table. Dylan put her slightly smushed cupcakes down next to a bowl of almonds and dried cranberries, a small mountain of Hershey bars, corn chips and salsa, Chips Ahoy and Oreos, and two bags of Starburst.

"Go ahead and eat," Patience invited. Dylan's teeth almost hurt from looking at all that sugar, but she ripped open the pack of Chips Ahoy, took three, and passed it around.

"No, thanks," Lynsey shook her head. She pulled out a granola bar from the pocket of her lavender velour pyjamas and peeled it open, looking virtuous. Dylan caught Lani's eye and shrugged.

"Let's start," Patience said, patting the space next to her on the bed for Lynsey and Honey to sit down. Alexandra, Malory, and Wei Lin were sitting cross-legged next to Razina on her bed. Lani was lying stretched out on the remaining bed, resting her chin on her hands. She pulled herself up to make room for Dylan.

"So," Lynsey said, leaning forward. "Who's going first?"

"I think Patience should, since it was her idea," said Alexandra, cleaning her glasses on the sleeve of her flannel robe.

"Does it have to be truth-or-dare?" Malory asked. "Can't we do something else, like tell ghost stories?"

"Ghost stories are so juvenile," Lynsey said scornfully.

"You got something against truth-or-dare, Malory? We'll all start thinking you have something to hide," Lani teased, stretching for an Oreo. "Did you bring the cupcakes, Dyl? There are only six. Do we split them or can I have a whole one?"

"Take a whole one," Patience urged. "You can have my half. Just don't leave crumbs. I don't want any bugs."

"I'll start," Lynsey said impatiently. "Once Dylan and Lani start talking about food, there'll be no stopping them." She looked across at Wei Lin. "Truth or dare?"

Wei Lin sat up, surprised to be the first up. "Truth," she said after some contemplation. She secured the tie on her silk polka-dot robe and leaned forward to hear her question.

"What's the most money you've ever spent on a pair of shoes?" Lynsey demanded.

"What kind of a question is that?" Lani protested.

"She chose truth," Lynsey reminded her.

"Five hundred dollars," Wei Lin admitted. "And they were secondhand."

"Who'd you buy them from? Elvis?" Honey blurted, her eyes wide.

"It was a charity bash – raising funds for orphaned children in Mexico. It's something my mom really believes in," Wei Lin began, not the least bit embarrassed. "Anyway, celebrities donate their shoes. And my mom bought a pair for me."

"No way!" Lynsey exclaimed, sounding horrified.

Dylan raised an eyebrow. She couldn't believe that Lynsey would think five hundred dollars was a lot to spend on a pair of shoes – at least not judging by the labels in her dirty clothes hamper.

"How come my mom wasn't involved with that event?" Lynsey went on indignantly. "She's on the board of three major children's charities and she misses one with celebrity shoes?"

"Well, the auction was in L.A.," Wei Lin told her.

"Oh," Lynsey said, losing interest, like anything on the West Coast didn't figure in her social orbit.

"So whose shoes did you get?" Patience demanded.

"Drew Barrymore's, I think – or maybe Cameron Diaz?" Wei Lin frowned. "I can't remember now. But the shoes were totally fabulous! They were limited edition Manolo Blahniks, but the bad news is that they were way too big, so my mom donated them to another charity and promised to buy me my own pair." She looked across at Razina and smiled. "I think I'm off the hook, so – Razina, truth or dare?"

Razina hiccupped as she said, "Dare. No, truth!"

"OK, then. Have you ever gone on a date?" Wei Lin

asked. "An official date."

From the way Razina's high cheekbones coloured, it was obvious that they were in store for some juicy gossip.

"Come on, Raz. Fess up," Patience whispered, suddenly sounding chummy.

Razina tipped her head to one side and bit her lower lip. "Is someone at the door?"

Everyone froze and stared at the door, expecting to see the handle turn at any moment. Dylan, who was closest, leaned down to see if she could see the shadow of feet under the door and soon realized they'd been tricked. "Razina," she whispered dramatically. "You don't get off the hook that easily."

"OK, OK!" Razina held up her hands. "There's this guy named Marcus who's in ninth grade. I met him because his dad is an exporter my mom works with."

"So, where'd you meet him?" Lynsey asked eagerly, hugging her knees.

"In a warehouse – not the most romantic of settings, I know!" Razina rolled her eyes.

"Where did you go on your date?" Patience wanted to know.

"It wasn't exactly a date," Razina confessed. "He came to my mom's gallery in New York, and we went for a walk in Central Park and then for coffee after. But it was at the end of the summer and I haven't seen him since. I'm not even sure my parents would let me go on an official date."

"Have you called him since you got here?" Lani asked.

Razina smiled. "Not yet. But I emailed him a few times. And he's written back twice."

"No way!" Lynsey exclaimed. "What does he write?"

Razina's cheeks darkened. "No, that's enough, I'm done now. Your turn, Mal. Truth or dare?"

Malory took a deep breath. "Sorry, guys, but I'd rather sit this one out."

Dylan frowned. *What was it with Malory? Why did she have to be so private?*

"Do you have some deep dark secret you don't want to let us in on?" Lani voiced Dylan's thoughts. "If you do, you really should think about playing – confession's good for the soul and all that."

"No, really. I'm fine listening," Malory protested, her voice apologetic but determined.

"Well, if we all thought that, there'd be no game," Lynsey said dismissively. "You'll have to ask someone else, Raz."

Malory looked down at her hands, but not before Dylan had noticed the relief in her eyes. *What is the deal with her?* she wondered as Razina threw down the challenge to Lynsey.

"Dare," Lynsey said, the corners of her lips slowly curling.

Razina's dark eyes gleamed. "I dare you to sneak down to the foyer and bring back a leaf from one of the potted plants."

Dylan was glad someone finally chose something other than truth, but she thought the dare was a little lame.

Patience, however, was grimacing and shaking her head. "You are allowed to appeal against your dare," she said. "It's a bit risky leaving the floor."

Lynsey tossed her hair over her shoulder. "Give me some credit! I'll be back in two minutes. Time me if you like." She slipped off the bed and tiptoed across the room. She glanced back at the girls with a grin before slipping out the door.

The stunned silence in the room was broken by Honey. "She didn't even take the flashlight."

"If she falls down the stairs and breaks a leg, do you think she'll let me ride Bluegrass for the tryouts?" Lani suggested, making Dylan stifle a laugh.

"I don't think that's very funny," Patience said when Dylan and Lani had recovered. "Chestnut Hill needs Lynsey on the team."

Dylan rolled her eyes. It seemed that Patience had appointed herself president of Lynsey's fan club. Dylan realized that she had not seen much of Patience without Lynsey around. And in her in a deep-pink velour track suit, she looked like a brunette clone of Lynsey. Even though Patience was the only other Adams girl in Dylan's English class, the two hadn't really talked. Patience was quiet during the lectures and usually left as soon as the bell rang.

By the time five minutes had passed and Lynsey still hadn't returned, the girls were all beginning to feel anxious. When the door opened a crack and a large, waxy leaf waved through the gap, Dylan felt a flood of relief.

Lynsey stepped inside the door and took a sweeping bow.

"What took you so long?" Patience worried. "My heart was pounding. Are you OK?"

Lynsey shrugged. "I thought I heard a noise, so I crawled up on the windowsill at the end of the hallway and hid behind the curtains."

"What was it?" asked Alexandra.

Lynsey shrugged. "Maybe nothing, but I waited a couple of minutes to make sure no one was there. That's it for me, then." She looked at Dylan. "Truth or dare?"

"Dare," Dylan said, raising her chin.

Lynsey smiled and carefully dropped the leaf in the wastepaper basket. "I dare you to take Morello around the last half of the course that Ms Carmichael wouldn't let you finish earlier today."

The mood in the room changed like someone had flipped a switch. "Come on," Honey said. "That's hardly the same as stealing a leaf!"

Lynsey shrugged and looked at Dylan. "Of course, if you and Morello aren't up to it. . ."

Dylan took a breath and closed her eyes. She'd had enough of Lynsey making smart remarks about Morello. This was a direct challenge. Before common sense had the chance to weigh in, Dylan impulsively jumped to her feet. "You're on!"

Chapter Nine

"You're crazy! You can't really do that!" Malory exclaimed.

Dylan ignored her. "I just have to change into my jodhpurs. I'll meet you at the jumping ring in ten minutes." Her heart was pounding, but there was no way she was backing down now.

"No offence, but I don't think I'll come. This is taking things too far," Razina said with certainty.

Dylan shrugged. "That's fine. No one else should have to risk getting caught for my dare."

"This is insane! What about Morello?" Malory insisted. "Have you thought what it'll be like for him being dragged out of his stall and forced to jump in the middle of the night?" Her eyes were dark with anger.

Dylan felt her own temper flare. "I'll know if he's up for it!" she announced.

"Dylan, I'll come back to our room with you, but I won't go down to the ring," Honey said in a hushed voice. "Sorry if you think I'm bailing out on you."

"Like I said, it's cool," Dylan told her, forcing a smile. But the solemn expression on Honey's face rattled her. *At least there'll be less chance of getting caught if it's just Lynsey and me down there*, she thought, trying not to panic.

"I'm going back to my room," Malory said. She got up and went to the door, followed by Alexandra. Malory looked back at Lani. "Are you coming?"

"You've gotta be kidding, right? I haven't had this much fun since my cousin entered his first rodeo!" Lani grinned at Dylan. "I'll be waiting down there, ready to cheer you on."

"Just as long as you keep it quiet," Dylan told her, feeling a guilty pang of relief that she wasn't going to be on her own after all. She waited for Malory and Alexandra to leave and then headed back to her own room, where the adrenaline rush that had been quieting her fears soon disappeared.

The moon was high and full, spilling light on the path to the stable yard. While Dylan was comforted by the fact that it was easy to see, she also realized that it would make it easy to be seen as well. As she neared the stable, she cast a nervous glance over her shoulder toward the dorm house. She had arranged to meet the others at the ring in ten minutes, which meant she didn't have much time to get Morello ready. Dylan cut off the path and jogged over the last stretch of lawn, relieved to see that her aunt's house, set deep in the trees at the far end of the yard, was in darkness.

She pulled back one of the barn doors and winced at the creaking hinges. It was a grinding, metallic sound – so distinct, she thought she'd recognize it anywhere. She hovered in the doorway, wondering if she should risk turning the lights on. She decided against it. The horses might think it was morning and start up a chorus of whinnies, anticipating their breakfast.

She hurried along the aisle, keeping the flashlight pointed down on the concrete floor. She went to the tack room first to fetch Morello's bridle and saddle, clenching the light between her neck and shoulder so she could use both hands.

Dylan then crossed to Morello's stall and pulled back the bolt. Focusing the flashlight beam on the ground, she found that the paint gelding was lying down with his front legs tucked underneath his chest. He blinked sleepily at Dylan and scrambled to his feet with a disoriented groan.

"Come on, sleepyhead," she said, unbuckling his sheet. "We're going to have some fun!"

Dylan couldn't believe how loud Morello's hooves sounded as they clattered out of the barn. Each step punctuated the silence of the night, reminding her that she was breaking an unlimited number of school rules.

She glanced at her watch and saw that she had taken a full fifteen minutes since leaving the dorm. Lani, Wei Lin, Lynsey, and Patience were all waiting by the arena gate, and Morello pricked his ears when he saw them.

Please don't call out to them, Dylan thought frantically, covering his nose.

She halted him outside the gate and checked her girth before swinging onto his back. Instinctively, she gave him a pat.

"Go easy," Lani told her, sounding serious for once. "If you don't think it's safe to jump, then pull up." The moonlight made her face look ghostly as she stood back for Dylan to enter the arena.

Dylan squeezed the gelding closer to the jumps, giving him a chance to get a good sense of his surroundings. It didn't take long for her to realize that, even with the moon, she couldn't see clearly enough to jump Morello safely. "We need more light," she whispered, turning Morello back to face the group.

"You wouldn't be trying to back out on your dare, would you?" Lynsey said, her voice uncomfortably loud.

"Of course not!" Dylan snapped. "I don't want to risk hurting Morello."

"I think we should go get the forklift from the barn, drive it down here and shine the headlights on the jumps," Lani said.

Lynsey tossed her head. "If you want us all to get caught, why don't you just turn on the floodlights and use the loudspeaker to announce what Dylan's doing?"

"I was making a joke," Lani said defiantly.

"What if we just went back to the dorm to get more flashlights?" Patience suggested.

"You know, you guys, if we get away with this, it will

be an absolute miracle," Wei Lin whispered, her eyes glinting like a cat's in the half-light.

"Well, if it's the only way she's going to do it…" Lynsey asserted. She was just short of accusing Dylan of fabricating unreasonable excuses to shirk her dare.

"We won't be long," Wei Lin promised over her shoulder as the girls hurried back toward the dorm, quickly vanishing into the shadows.

Dylan nudged Morello to walk around the ring so he wouldn't get antsy. Her teeth were chattering, but she had the suspicion that it was from her nerves rather than the damp autumn night. Still, she had only stopped long enough to pull her jods on, and her fitted pyjama top was a thin layer against the chill. As she walked, she reconsidered the situation. She was insane to have agreed to this. Riding without a trainer and without permission was one thing – riding without light was suicidal.

She leaned forward and slipped her arms around Morello's warm neck. "I'm so sorry, boy," she murmured into his mane. "Please help me get us through this, and I promise I'll never do anything so stupid again."

Morello's ear flickered back and he snorted, his breath making clouds that faded into the black night.

When Dylan caught sight of three flashlights bobbing toward the arena, she straightened up and shortened her reins. Her heart was pounding so hard that the sound filled her ears, and she felt nauseous as she pushed Morello into a trot.

Lynsey, Patience, Lani, and Wei Lin stood by the

fence and aimed their flashlights at the red-and-white parallel bars of the first jump. The beams illuminated the area surrounding the fence, giving Dylan added confidence. She could do this. She nudged Morello with her heel, and he eased into an even, lively canter. Dylan sat back and tried to settle in with his rhythm. As she turned Morello toward the fence, his ears pricked and he sprang forward. Morello didn't falter as he gathered himself and took the jump with an eager leap. Dylan's heart surged with love for the brave pony. He was so willing and generous, despite the odd circumstances. She knew Morello would show them all.

They landed smoothly, and Dylan was sure she heard Lani give a hushed cheer as she turned Morello toward the next jump, which was five strides away.

Suddenly, the lights all veered from the pony's path and the ring was absorbed by darkness. Dylan pulled hard on the reins as the jump disappeared before her. Morello skidded to a halt, and she waited for her eyes to adjust.

"Dylan Walsh! Get off that pony – immediately!"

Dylan forced some cereal into her mouth and tried to concentrate on chewing. As soon as breakfast was over, she was headed for Dr Starling's office. Dylan was certain that a nine o'clock appointment on a Saturday wasn't the best way to formally meet your principal. The cafeteria was almost deserted since most of the other girls were enjoying the chance to sleep in. There was a selection of cereal and fruit for students who were up early for approved extracurricular activities. Somehow, Dylan knew midnight jumping courses were not on the list.

Both her aunt and Mrs Herson had been furious. They had shown up at the arena at the same time. Once Ali had ordered Dylan off Morello, Mrs Herson marched her and the others back to the dorm. She had had few words for Dylan, but she made it clear that she would be expected outside the principal's office at nine sharp.

Dylan had hardly slept all night.

She didn't notice Lynsey and Patience sitting down next to her until Lynsey bent her head close to Dylan's and whispered, "Thanks for not saying that I dared you to ride Morello."

Dylan looked up from her bowl. "Aren't you guys up kind of early for a Saturday?"

"Are you kidding? We couldn't let you be on your own after what happened last night," Lynsey said. "So, what did Mrs Herson say? Do you have to meet with Dr Starling?"

"Right after I've eaten this." Dylan nodded at her cereal.

"Are you going to tell her everything that happened last night?" Patience asked, drawing a circle on the table with her finger.

Dylan shrugged. "You mean about the game? I can't see the point in getting anyone else busted."

"Dylan, I feel really bad," Lynsey said, pressing her hands against her cheeks. "I didn't really think about what would happen if you took me up on that stupid dare. I never thought you'd do it."

"Well, I proved you wrong," Dylan said with little satisfaction. She knew Lynsey and Patience were there to convince her not to turn them in, and it would probably work. She wondered if she would get any leniency if she told the whole truth. "Besides, you didn't make me do it. It was my decision. I rode Morello without permission, so I'm the one who should pay for it." Dylan knew it was true. She had no one to blame but herself. She was the one who couldn't stand up to Lynsey. She was the one who did not want to back down on a dare.

"I just hope you don't end up being expelled. We'd really miss you – wouldn't we?" Lynsey looked at Patience, who nodded.

Dylan shoved her bowl away, knowing she couldn't eat a bite more. Already, her stomach was churning with nerves. She forced herself to smile at her table companions. "Well, if my only punishment is cleaning the student centre bathrooms for three weeks, I'll give you both some Lysol and assign you a stall," she said, standing up.

"Good luck," Lynsey and Patience called after her. But Dylan didn't look back. The inside of her mouth was totally dry and the churning in her gut felt like it was steadily expanding to the rest of her body. At that point, she would be willing to clean all the bathrooms on campus for the remainder of the year if she could somehow avoid getting expelled from Chestnut Hill.

* * *

Dylan waited in the seating area outside Dr Starling's office, staring at the plaid of her uniform skirt. She decided that was far more comforting than looking at the portraits of past principals that were hanging on the walls, their eyes looking down on her in dismay.

And Mrs Danby, the principal's assistant, was giving off judgmental vibes as well. She sat behind her desk, reading, but Dylan noted that she hadn't spoken a word to her except when she directed her to sit down and wait. Dylan wondered if the administrative staff always worked on Saturday mornings.

Folding her hands in her lap, she ran her eyes over the books on the oak shelves. It was a pretty impressive collection, with Shakespeare's complete works, Tolstoy's *War and Peace*, Tolkien's *The Hobbit*, and various poetry anthologies lining the top row. Before Dylan had the chance to scan other shelves or wonder who actually read these books, the door to Dr Starling's room clicked open and Dylan's housemother came out. Dylan swallowed. She'd never have guessed that Mrs Herson's brown eyes could look so expressionless, so cold.

"You can come in now," Mrs Herson said.

Dylan trailed after her into a beautiful, wood-panelled room that was flooded with morning sunlight. The principal waved her hand for Dylan to enter. There were three chairs in front of Dr Starling's desk; her aunt was sitting in one, but she didn't turn her head as Dylan stepped forward. Dylan hovered uncertainly, not knowing if she should sit or stay standing.

"Sit down, Dylan," Dr Starling said.

Dylan sat on the edge of the empty chair in between Mrs Herson and Ali. She felt more and more anxious as Dr Starling closed a blue file on her desk and stood up to put it away in a cabinet. She wouldn't have bet in a million years that, only three weeks into the semester, she would have been sitting here in the principal's office. Dylan looked out of the huge windows, which were framed by long cream drapes. She wished with all her heart that she was outside, riding over the distant hills, miles away from all this trouble. Her eyes wandered to a beautiful framed charcoal sketch of a horse's head that hung over the mantelpiece just behind the desk. Dylan wondered if that was Dr Starling's horse. Everyone knew that the principal was a dedicated horsewoman who took personal pride in the success of Chestnut Hill's programme. Dr Starling certainly wouldn't have ridden a horse over a course of fences in the middle of the night. Who would do that? Dylan felt she could no longer relate to the person who had made that steady string of bad decisions the night before. What had she been thinking?

The sound of the filing cabinet closing startled her, and she looked up nervously as the principal lowered herself into her high-backed chair. "I'm going to cut to the chase with you, Dylan," she said, picking up her pen and holding it at both ends. "We're all incredibly disappointed in your actions last night."

Dylan's chest felt hollow, as if she could hardly get a breath. She bowed her head, feeling her cheeks burn with shame.

"It wasn't just that you broke school rules," Dr Starling continued without raising her voice. "You broke something far more valuable." Dylan glanced up, concerned that something awful had happened to Morello after all. "You broke the bond of trust that is given to every girl at Chestnut Hill," Dr Starling carried on, her grey eyes fixed on Dylan. "And once that trust is broken, it is my decision whether it can be granted a second time."

Dylan's heart began to race. *Well, that's it,* she thought frantically. *This is the moment when I get kicked out of boarding school for playing truth-or-dare.* What would her parents say? Considering how hard her aunt had been on her this semester, she wouldn't have been surprised if Ali had already called them with the stellar news.

"I've spoken with Ms Carmichael and Mrs Herson." Dr Starling glanced at them both. "They have given you excellent references and neither can understand why you pulled that stunt last night or what might have made you think it was a good idea. Really, Dylan, jumping in the dark is not something an intelligent or rational student would do." She paused, and it was clear she was waiting for Dylan to offer an explanation – some proof that she was either intelligent or rational.

Dylan twisted her hands in her lap. This was about the worst she had ever felt, and there was no way she was going to put anyone else through this interrogation. Of course, it was tempting to admit that she hadn't dreamed up the insane scheme on her own, but she knew she had to take the full blame. "It was all my fault," she said. "I totally messed up, and all I can say is that I'm really sorry." This time she didn't look away from Dr Starling's piercing gaze. This was her plea, short but sincere.

"You should know, Dylan, that Ms Carmichael has spoken quite passionately in your defence. She explained that you spent quite some time riding Morello this summer and that you formed a real bond with him. She feels this is one of the reasons that you acted the way you did. She also feels you wouldn't have taken any of the other horses here and ridden them without permission, unsupervised, and at such an hour."

Dylan felt a surge of gratitude toward her aunt. She had not expected Ali to take her side, but what she had said was true.

"Nevertheless, this doesn't take away from the fact that what you did wasn't just breaking the rules, it was downright dangerous." Dr Starling began tapping the desk with her pen. "I've checked your references from your old school and they describe you as a mature, conscientious student, and Mrs Herson echoes that. And it's because of this that I've decided to give you one more chance to prove yourself."

Dylan sat expressionless and let the words sink in, feeling a small seed of hope start to swell in her chest.

Then, all at once, she thought she would yelp for joy.

But Dr Starling was still looking at her seriously, and Dylan was determined to prove her dedication by giving the principal her full attention. "That said, I'm sure you understand that you still have to be punished for what you did last night. Nothing so drastic can go undisciplined. After discussing the situation with Ms Carmichael and Mrs Herson, I've decided that you should complete a week of afternoon and evening detentions." She paused and leaned forward, pressing her fingertips together. "And no riding for two weeks, starting today."

Chapter Ten

Dylan felt as if an electric shock had just jolted through her body. She stood up, her heart pounding. "No riding for two weeks? What about the tryouts?"

"Dylan, sit down!" Ali Carmichael said sharply, to remind her that she was in the principal's office and should show some respect.

"But the tryouts," Dylan protested. "Please! Getting onto the junior team is all I care about."

"Now, Dylan," Mrs Herson warned. "Surely your commitment to Chestnut Hill goes beyond the riding team."

Dylan slumped back into her chair. *This is a total nightmare*, she thought. She stared at the blue carpet until it began to blur. *Except it is worse than anything my subconscious could create.* She wrapped her arms around her stomach, swallowing her feeling of nausea. She glanced up, and her eyes fell on the school motto mounted on a gold plaque on Dr Starling's desk. *Veritas, Sapientia, Fides.* It was Latin for Truth, Wisdom,

Loyalty. She shook her head. *Yeah, right.* If she'd had a little more wisdom last night, then she would have chosen truth instead of dare, and she wouldn't be in this trouble now. And no matter what she had said to Lynsey earlier, Dylan didn't think the nature of her roommate's dare had shown much loyalty, either.

Ali Carmichael cleared her throat. "What you have to understand is that both you and Morello were very lucky not to have had a serious accident with that stunt you pulled last night. I asked you to stop jumping Morello in your lesson yesterday because he had already completed a class. You didn't seem to have trouble putting his needs first then. No one is impressed by a show-off. And I, personally, cannot tolerate one, especially when she endangers the safety of one of my horses."

Dylan's fingers tightened. It hadn't been like that at all! She bit down hard on her lip, knowing that if she talked back, her relatively tame punishment might be exchanged for a much more severe one. She concentrated instead on the thought that, even with the two-week ban, she would still have a short window of time to get ready for the tryouts.

Dylan left Dr Starling's office feeling lost. She was longing to go down to the stables to give Morello a huge hug and make sure that he was OK after she'd dragged him out in the middle of the night. But she wasn't allowed to go to the stables while she was in detention. The idea of going a whole Saturday without being able to hang out on the yard was totally unthinkable. For once, Dylan wished her dorm weren't so tantalizingly close to the stables.

"Dylan!" Lynsey was peering around the corner of the first-floor hallway of Adams, waving her fingers.

Dylan made her way over. The way Lynsey was acting, she looked like she was trying out for a role in the latest Bond movie.

"What's with all the secrecy?" she asked.

"Come on, Dylan," Patience said. "What did Starling say? Are we all busted?"

"I told you I wasn't going to get anyone else in trouble," Dylan said scornfully. Then she looked at them questioningly. "I am kind of surprised that I'm the only one who has to go see her. I mean, I wasn't going to say anything, but Mrs Herson knows I wasn't the only one down at the ring... Granted, I was the only one cantering over verticals."

"Maybe we'll get called in later," Lynsey interrupted, taking Dylan's arm and pulling her across the foyer. "Come on, you have to tell us what happened. Everyone's waiting!"

Wei Lin and Razina abandoned their game of chess when Dylan and Lynsey walked into the sitting room. "Over here." Lani waved, pulling out her iPod earphones. She patted the sofa beside her.

Alexandra closed her book and put it down on the table. It was one of their assigned titles, *The Color Purple*. "How did it go?"

"It could have been worse, I guess," Dylan said, sitting next to Lani and tucking her feet up. "I didn't get expelled, at least."

"So, what did you get?" Lynsey asked, her voice loaded with sympathy as she sat down on the opposite sofa. Patience and Honey switched off MTV-2 on the plasma screen and came across to listen.

Dylan noticed that Malory wasn't around, but apart from that, it seemed everyone had hung around to see her. "I never thought last night would turn me into a celebrity!" she joked. "But I guess it's more like being on the cover of *National Enquirer* than *Vogue*."

"Come on, tell us what happened," Wei Lin said.

"I have a week of afternoon and evening detention," Dylan announced. "And I've been banned from riding for two weeks."

Lani gasped. "You must be freaking out!"

"Pretty much," Dylan admitted.

"Wow, that doesn't leave you much time. Tryouts are the week after," Lynsey murmured. "Dylan, I'm sorry I gave you that stupid dare. I was originally going to make you eat three of those smashed cupcakes."

"Yeah, were you going to lace them with arsenic?" Lani asked drily, and Lynsey shot back a look of genuine hurt.

"What gets me is that nobody else has been busted. There were four of you who were out after curfew," Razina said, frowning.

Lynsey shrugged. "I guess Mrs Herson thought we were out looking for Dylan."

Razina stared at her. "You think? Lani said you were essentially lighting the course. Sounds like conspiracy to me."

"Maybe they wanted to limit the number of Saturday appointments," Wei Lin suggested. "I'm not sure we're in the clear."

"Well, I'd like to know who snitched," Lani said, looking around. "It was a pretty lousy thing to do, whoever it was."

"What makes you so sure that someone told on her?" Patience demanded.

"Oh, come on! Like Hersie woke up in the middle of the night, decided to check Dylan's room. Then, when she wasn't there, woke up Ms Carmichael and they knew to look in the jumping arena. If you believe that, I have to wonder how you passed the tests to get into this school," Lani said, her tone short and harsh. "It doesn't take much to figure it out."

"It was a dumb idea from the start. You're all lucky that nobody got hurt," said a new voice.

Dylan had been so caught up in what Lani was saying that she hadn't seen Malory come into the room.

She stared at her, and Malory met her gaze head-on. "I hope you realize how stupid it was trying to jump Morello in the middle of the night, now," she went on, refusing to drop her glare.

Dylan narrowed her eyes. Everyone in the room understood that it was stupid now. Why did Malory feel the need to point it out? Dylan had a sudden suspicion that the snitch was standing in front of her.

"Was that what you said to Mrs Herson? 'Dylan had this dumb idea to jump Morello in the middle of the night. Go and see for yourself!' "

"Dylan," Razina said in a cautionary tone.

"At least with Mrs Herson finding out, Morello didn't get hurt, crashing into a fence that he couldn't even see," Malory said, crossing her arms.

"I can't believe you!" Dylan snapped, getting to her feet. "Do you always have to be right? From the start of semester, you've acted like you're better than the rest of us. You'd rather clean tack than watch movies, you sit out truth-or-dare. Does winning the Rockwell Award make you too good to be one of us?"

Malory's cheeks drained, and her blue eyes were bright with moisture. Without saying another word, she spun on her heel and walked out of the room, banging the door.

"Well." Lynsey broke the silence. "I'm glad you weren't expelled, Dylan. I don't know what we'd have done for entertainment without you around."

Later that evening, Dylan wandered down to the lake and pulled out her cell phone to call Nat. She gazed across the silvery water while the phone rang, watching the pale sunlight dance across the surface. Tiny dragonflies flitted just above the water, disappearing when two swans left the sloping lawn to glide into the shallows.

With each unanswered ring, Dylan felt a deeper pang of rejection. She had already called her parents and tried to explain her side of the story. She didn't want them to find out that she was an irrational show-off from anyone else – particularly if that someone was Ali Carmichael. Not surprisingly, Dylan's dad was disappointed. Dylan was certain he had read in some psychology book that being "disappointed" with your child made much more of an impression than being angry, and he was right. It had been awful telling him, but, after Dylan had sputtered out all the details, he seemed to understand the circumstances that had led to her "unacceptably impulsive behavior," to use his exact words. Her mom, however, declared that she wanted Dylan to report all of the other girls who played truth-or-dare. It had taken both Dylan and her dad to convince Mrs Walsh that it was in her daughter's best interest to refrain from telling Dr Starling of the other students' involvement.

Dylan really needed to talk to someone who knew her well – someone who wasn't investing in her private school education. She could call one of her friends from home, but she had decided her best bet was to dial Nat. Just as she was about to hang up, Dylan heard a click.

"Hey, what's going on?" Nat asked.

"Um, not much," Dylan responded, knowing that any other Saturday she would be far too busy to call him. She'd either have gone into town with friends or be hanging out in the stable, but she was currently suspended from both activities.

"Huh." Nat sounded distracted. "Do you want me to believe that? Or do you want to talk about it?"

"Don't tell me you already know," Dylan said to her cousin. She plucked a blade of fresh-cut grass from the lawn and started to pull it apart along one of its seams.

"I could lie to you," he said dryly. "Would that help?"

"Nat! Do you have to be such a jerk?" Dylan heard an elongated sigh from the other end of the line. She hated when her cousin played coy.

"No, I guess not," he replied with another sigh. "OK, I have to be honest with you, Dylan. I heard my mom's version of the story at three o'clock this morning. She was really worried, wondering if she would get fired. She said she knew she had been hard on you over the past weeks because she knows how good you are, and she wondered if you were trying to get back at her. She wouldn't normally call me about something like that, but she thought I might have some clue what was going on with you. I didn't. I couldn't think of a single thing that would make you do what you did."

Dylan was struck silent. Nat was the last person she had expected to give her a lecture. She had heard her parents talk about some of the things he had gotten into with his friends from Kentucky, but he obviously saw the situation with Dylan differently. He had been very protective of his mom since she and his dad had gotten divorced. Dylan guessed he couldn't see her dare as just another petty prank because he was so concerned about how it would affect his mom.

"Well, that's how I found out," Nat continued. "I guess it's only fair to hear your side, too."

Dylan hesitated, not certain she should unload

anything else on her cousin. Still, she wanted him to know that it wasn't some master plan that she had engineered – and she certainly hadn't meant to get Ali in trouble. "It was so stupid," she began, being careful not to mention any names. "I have been frustrated with Aunt Ali, but that's not what it was about." She knew Nat wouldn't say anything to his mom, but she wanted to minimize the social damage. It was her tale to tell, and she did just that, recounting every sorry scene.

"Well," Nat said when Dylan finished, "that does sound stupid."

"Thanks a lot," Dylan replied, but she could tell that Nat's tone wasn't incriminating. He now sounded like he was in on the joke, willing to laugh at Dylan's predicament rather than judge her for it.

"I totally get how you were pulled in, though. An outright dare is hard to resist," Nat sympathized. "And now you're on detention duty for a week?"

"Yeah, and no riding until the week of tryouts."

"That bites. I'm sorry. Do you want to try to meet up next Saturday? You'll be stir crazy by then. Maybe we can see a movie to keep your mind off everything?"

"That would be great, Nat. Thanks." Dylan was relieved that he understood after all. Seeing him would be something to look forward to as she sat through the endless days of detention. After she hung up, she tossed a pebble into the lake, watching the ripples spreading out on top of the surface. She couldn't help but think of the night before, and how one bad decision had caused so many aftershocks. Deep down, she knew she was lucky to have gotten off with just a two-week ban. It could have been much, much worse. But, still, she couldn't wait for all this to be over and things to return to normal.

By Wednesday, Dylan was all caught up in her classes. Sitting alone in a room left her little to do other than homework and reading. If it weren't for the staff monitor who checked in at random intervals, Dylan would have been IMing everyone in her address book, but she didn't want to get caught and get her sentence doubled. The worst part was that she was in Room Eleven of the liberal arts hall – the room that looked directly at the back of the stables. Dylan could see the length of the closest barn as well as the muck heap, but she couldn't catch a glimpse of the paddocks or the riding arena from any desk – and not for lack of trying.

The first half of the week had been even longer than she had anticipated. After her sitting-room reception on Saturday, not that many people had talked with her. Dylan didn't think that they were trying to ignore her. It was more like they didn't have anything to say – not even Honey and Lani. She had overheard several conversations about the courses Ali had set up for the intermediates, but the discussion had drawn to a quick close as soon as Dylan came near.

As for Malory, she was nowhere in sight. *She's probably busy shaking out every single saddle pad in the stable or picking lint off of Ali's hard hat*, Dylan thought. But even as she lingered on the thought, trying to get satisfaction from her momentary cruelty, Dylan felt a pang of disenchantment. She had really liked Malory at the start. Sure, the other girl had seemed closed off about her personal life, but she was still fun. Dylan pictured Malory crawling along the paddock ground, trying to tempt Nutmeg into letting her put the halter on. That day had felt so new, so full of possibilities. So how did Dylan find her way to Room Eleven and a permanent record?

All she could do was to check the syllabus of every class and do her best to get ahead. Then, as soon as she was able to get back in the saddle again, she could concentrate fully on the tryouts and not let coursework get in the way. That was her best chance, maybe her only one.

Dylan pressed her forehead against the van window. After a week of double detention, she felt like she had been in an isolation chamber! She was just relieved to be looking out the window and seeing something besides a manure pile. She'd be happy if she never set foot in Room Eleven again. *Still*, she thought, watching the cars on the opposite side of the road zip by, *at least Lynsey's been pretty cool through all this. That's a huge improvement*. She glanced down at the silky oyster-coloured Versace T shirt her roommate had loaned her for the trip into town. The term "T-shirt" hardly did this garment justice. It had gold embroidered detailing around the collar and cap sleeves and asymmetrical pleats down the front. Lynsey had insisted Dylan borrow something festive to celebrate her halfway mark to freedom – one more week and she'd have full riding privileges again. Dylan smoothed the supple fabric. The shirt was brand-new. Lynsey had cut the tags off before handing it over. All week it had felt as if Lynsey was trying to make up for giving Dylan the dare in the first place. She had even agreed to take carrots to Morello! Dylan was starting to think she'd gotten Lynsey all wrong. She was showing potential for being a good friend after all.

Lynsey's attitude adjustment was good news, but what made Dylan truly happy was Morello.

She smiled, remembering that morning. Before breakfast, she had raced down to the stable to see him, and he had greeted her with an exuberant whinny. It seemed his loyalties were still firmly with Dylan despite Lynsey's carrot offerings. Having to tell Morello that she still couldn't ride nearly broke her heart, but she was glad that she was no longer banned from the barn.

"Do you guys want to come bowling with us later?" Lynsey turned around in the seat she was sharing with Patience.

"Thanks, but I don't think we'll have time to do that and still catch a movie," Dylan replied. She glanced over at Honey and smiled. The school rule was that they could only go into town in groups of three or more, and Honey was part of Lynsey's crew. Dylan was relieved when Razina and Wei Lin had been game to hang out with her and meet up with Nat because they had wanted to catch a movie themselves.

"OK." Lynsey shrugged. "If you change your mind, call my cell."

The van stopped outside Starbucks, at the far end of the sprawling outdoor mall. Before Dylan even stepped onto the sidewalk, the rich smell of coffee mixed with baked goods hit her, making her mouth water. *First stop, coffee and calories,* she thought, taking in another breath of autumn air. "Hey, can you guys handle a caffeine jolt?" she asked Wei Lin and Razina.

"Are you kidding? I can't remember the last time I had a decent latte." Razina laughed.

"It wouldn't happen to have been at a certain coffee shop in New York?" Dylan teased, remembering Razina's confession about her date at the end of the summer. She grinned at Wei Lin as Razina headed toward the shop, struggling to suppress a smile.

Inside, a long line snaked past the glass display counter toward the back of the café. "Why don't you two grab those seats while I get in line?" Wei Lin suggested.

"You don't mind?" Razina hesitated.

"Go!" Wei Lin flapped her hand.

Dylan quickly gave Wei Lin her order and rushed after Razina.

"You wanted a large green tea, right?" Dylan playfully asked Razina as soon as they were settled on their stools.

"What? Tea? No, I wanted a latte," Razina announced, making a move to storm Wei Lin in line. Dylan broke out in laughter. Razina was very confident

147

and bordered on being too serious, so Dylan took special pleasure in teasing her. Razina's jaw dropped when she realized Dylan had tricked her again.

"Really," Dylan declared, "for someone so smart, you fall for a lot of stupid jokes."

"Thanks, Dylan," Razina said, tossing her braids so they fell evenly down her back. "For someone so smart, you pull a lot of dumb pranks."

While Dylan took Razina's jab as an offhand compliment, she also assumed the girl had been referring to the truth-or-dare debacle. It would be a long time before she lived that down.

All of a sudden, Razina's eyes widened with alarm as she looked over Dylan's shoulder. "Watch out!" she warned.

"You'll have to try harder than that," Dylan grinned, unwilling to fall for such an obvious trick. But a moment later, she wished she hadn't laughed off Razina's warning. She suddenly felt a freezing sensation ooze through her T-shirt – correction, Lynsey's T-shirt. Dylan looked down, catching her breath in horror as she watched half-melted chocolate ice-cream drip down Lynsey's new Versace top.

"Oh, I'm so sorry!" the woman behind her said.

Dylan spun around to see a toddler waving an empty ice-cream cone in the air. A pair of blue eyes twinkled in a face that was almost completely covered in sticky chocolate. When the child realized her dessert was on the floor, she started to cry.

"Don't worry about it," Dylan said, trying to camouflage her frustration. She held up her hands in an attempt to stave off the woman, who looked as if she was about to attack Dylan with a tub of baby wipes. "These things happen, I guess." The words stuck in her throat as she pictured Lynsey's face when she returned her chocolate-stained top. She turned back to Razina, who was staring in horror at what had been a very stylish, very expensive shirt. "Any ideas on how to get ice cream out of Versace?"

"Sure. Put it in the trash and buy a new one on eBay," Razina said, dabbing at the huge dark stain with a napkin. "I don't think this is going to come out. Sorry."

"It's Lynsey's," Dylan told her. "I bet she's going to have a thing or two to say about it."

"When doesn't she?" Razina said, quitting her efforts and wiping her own hands with a napkin.

Dylan was surprised by Razina's comment. She had always thought that both Razina and Wei Lin liked Lynsey. They seemed to be two of the lucky few to have earned Lynsey's approval. "Actually she's been cool recently," Dylan pointed out charitably, realizing both Lynsey and Patience had been more supportive than anyone else that week.

"It's about time!" Razina's eyebrows shot up. "Lynsey's got enough nerve for our whole class. I'm surprised you're putting up with her at all."

"What?" Dylan felt confused. She looked over to see how Wei Lin was doing. She was still third in line. It looked like the guy at the counter was ordering for four tables.

"I don't think I'd be as forgiving if she'd gotten me a week of detentions and a riding ban," Razina said, pulling off her graphite-beaded cardigan and draping it over the back of her stool.

Dylan frowned. She hadn't counted on discussing conspiracy theories with Razina. "But that was Malory," she insisted.

"Really?" Razina looked doubtful. "I'm not so sure. Think about it. Lynsey was the one who gave you the dare in the first place. And I know Malory wasn't exactly encouraging you to take the bet, but she still doesn't seem like she'd rat you out. It's not her style."

Dylan stared out of the window at the crowded mall, not really seeing the shoppers as she turned Razina's words over in her head. "Malory as good as admitted that *she* did it," she protested.

"From where I was sitting, you told her she was a snitch and she didn't say she was or wasn't," Razina said quietly.

Dylan started shredding a paper napkin as her conscience began to nag at her. Razina was right about Malory not seeming the type to tattle.

Razina shrugged. "I could be wrong about it being Lynsey, but I'd bet my Gucci cocktail dress it wasn't Malory."

Dylan felt like her insides were going through a wringer. Could it have been Lynsey? She kept on trying to push the thought away, but each time she did, it came back stronger. And to think she'd actually been grateful for Lynsey's gestures that week. *Grateful! Hah!* Lynsey must have been rolling with laughter behind her back.

Dylan didn't like to feel gullible. Her fingers worked through the napkin until she had built a small mountain of shredded paper on the counter. "I just don't get why she'd do it," she said, trying to get a grip on the red-hot anger rising inside.

Razina shrugged. "I wondered that. I mean, I know the two of you haven't exactly been kindred spirits…"

Dylan looked long and hard at Razina. She thought that Razina was the only person who would describe her relationship with Lynsey that way. Everyone knew they struggled to be civil. Dylan wasn't sure why. It just seemed like it was easier to exchange snarky insults than say nothing at all. Dylan glanced down and screwed the napkin shreds into a ball. But it wasn't just that she hadn't bonded with Lynsey. She wasn't best friends yet with anyone in her class, even though she liked them all. Almost all, she corrected herself.

"Maybe she figured if you got busted you wouldn't be allowed to try out for the team," Razina said, jumping down from her stool to help Wei Lin, who was making her way toward them balancing a tray full of steaming cups and pastries. "You could even take it as a kind of compliment, I guess, if she felt threatened. I can't explain it, but I'm suspicious. I wouldn't put it past her."

In the back of her mind, Dylan thought that Lynsey was far too secure in her riding abilities to try to pick off competitors, but Dylan was too frustrated to think straight. She might not have a plan, but she wasn't going to let Lynsey believe she had gotten the best of Dylan Walsh.

Chapter Eleven

Dylan was still fuming as she walked to the movie theatre with Razina and Wei Lin. The more she thought about everything Razina had said, the more she suspected Lynsey was the one who had stabbed her in the back. *But if it was Lynsey, she didn't get what she really wanted – I'm still allowed to compete in the tryouts.*

At the theatre, she scanned the crowd for Nat. Finally she saw him standing near a small group close to the entrance. His red hair made him easy to find. Dylan recognized one of the two boys with Nat. It was Caleb, the cute guy who had been checking out Malory at the symposium. She hurried forward, anxious to tell Nat everything Razina had said and get his take, but she stopped abruptly. Straight ahead was the one person Dylan least wanted to see.

"Oh, great," she muttered, her defences going into overdrive. She started to button up her green suede jacket. She wanted to at least try to clean the T-shirt before Lynsey saw it.

"What's up?" Wei Lin asked. "Isn't your cousin here?"

"He's over there." Dylan pointed to the bench underneath one of the coming-attraction posters. "But I need to make a call before I go into the movie."

"That's cool. We'll go get the tickets," Razina said.

"Great. Thanks, guys," Dylan said. She wondered if there was any way to get through to Nat and tell him she couldn't handle sitting through the movie if Lynsey was going to tag along.

"Oh, hi, Dylan," Lynsey called, spotting her before Dylan could get Nat's attention. Dylan could not believe her luck. There was a massive swarm of people in front of the theatre. How had Lynsey noticed her? Dylan blamed her own red hair as she made her way through the crowd.

"I hope you don't mind us crashing, but we figured a movie sounded more fun than bowling," Lynsey explained, acting as the designated spokesperson for Patience and Honey as well.

Dylan wondered if her disappointment was obvious because, when Nat's eyes met hers, there seemed to be a hint of apology in them. "Dylan, this is Josh and Caleb." He introduced the two boys with him. Both had thick, short hair, but where Caleb's was dark, Josh's was a pale blond. "They heard I was planning to go to the movies today and begged me to let them tag along."

"What he really means is that he doesn't have any friends, so he paid us to look like we want to hang with him." Josh's green eyes crinkled at the corners. Dylan knew Saint Kit's had the same rule for a minimum of three students leaving campus when not accompanied by an adult.

"Hey, Dylan. You're not here on your own, are you?" Patience asked, stepping back to look for Dylan's off-campus companions.

"You know you'd get kicked out of school for sure if you got caught breaking rules a second time," Lynsey added. She smiled at Nat. "Dylan's on her best behavior at the moment."

"Really?" Nat raised his eyebrows at Dylan. "That sounds difficult for you."

"Well, you know me," Dylan told him, praying that he'd figure out what she was trying to do. "I took on this dumb dare to jump a pony at night, and I got caught. You know, misuse of school property and all."

"Whoa! Nat, does delinquency run in the family? We could do with a little more action at Saint Kit's," Caleb said, trying to ease the awkwardness after Dylan's confession.

Patience looked straight at the cute dark-haired boy. "I can't believe it's dull with you guys there."

Come on, Dylan thought. *Could Patience be any more obvious?*

"How'd you get busted?" Josh asked, feeding Dylan the perfect line.

"You know, I can't quite figure it out," she said. "I thought that our housemother had checked on us and seen our empty beds, but that doesn't really make any sense."

"What makes you say that?" Nat said helpfully.

"Because I wasn't the only one who went down to the ring. Lynsey and Patience were there, too," Dylan explained, looking her classmates in the eye. "There were five of us in all. Anyway, the weirdest thing was that it wasn't even our housemother who showed up first. It was the riding instructor," she continued with the boys' full attention, "and the other really weird thing was, before the instructor even got to the ring, before she could have seen who was riding, she yelled my name."

"Dude, you were set up!" Josh exclaimed. "That sucks."

"Sure sounds like it," Caleb agreed. "Do you know who turned you in?"

"She doesn't know," Lynsey blurted. "The instructor must have assumed it was Dylan because she was on the stable's only painted pony, which Dylan *loves* for some reason."

Just then, Honey clicked her cell phone closed and walked over to the group. "Sorry about that. Hey, Dylan," she said, smiling. But the atmosphere was crackling with negative vibes, and her smile quickly faded to a puzzled frown.

"That's a good point," Nat added, always wanting to consider all the possibilities. "A paint might show up in the dark."

"That sounds too convenient. I think that instructor knew exactly who was in the ring," Caleb offered.

"Well," Dylan said with a sigh, "I'm going to try not

to think about it. It isn't something you'd expect one of your friends to do."

"Some friend," Josh said, his voice heavy with irony.

"Yeah, that's low. So, do you know who it was?" Caleb ran his hand through his thick dark hair, and Patience's eyes widened so far that Dylan thought the rest of her face would disappear.

"I have some ideas," Dylan replied, "but I don't want to be a snitch, too."

"I don't understand," Honey ventured. Dylan looked at Honey's uncertain expression and felt bad for bringing her into this.

"I agree. Who would want to get you in trouble?" Lynsey absentmindedly pushed her purse up on her shoulder. "Besides, you only have a week left and you'll be riding again. What's important is that you weren't expelled."

Dylan thought Lynsey's comment sounded defensive.

"That's true. I'll be back in the saddle just in time for tryouts," she confirmed. "I know how worried you were about my missing them."

Lynsey's cheeks went pink under her Bobbi Brown blush. "You know, I've seen this movie already, so I think we'll go bowling after all," she said, brushing an imaginary piece of dust off her velveteen jacket. "Come on," she said to Patience and Honey, not waiting for them as she stalked off.

Honey stared after Lynsey, looking completely baffled. Patience bit down on her lip, clearly reluctant to lose her chance to be with Caleb. She glared at

Dylan, "What's the deal? Sometimes I wonder why Lynsey bothers being so nice to you."

She turned on her heel and hurried after her friend.

"Well, I guess I'll see you back at the van," Honey shrugged, turning to catch up with Lynsey and Patience, who were walking with their heads close together, deep in conversation.

Nat waited for Honey to get out of earshot and then looked at Dylan, his amber eyes dancing. "I don't remember telling her what movie we were going to see."

"Oh, that's too bad," Dylan dramatized. "I was so looking forward to spending more time with her."

Dylan stared down at the hot plates. "I've died and gone to heaven," she murmured to Honey. On Sundays the girls had brunch instead of a separate breakfast and lunch, and Dylan hadn't been too thrilled to be losing one meal out of a day at first. But now she was a convert. Hash browns, grits, tomatoes, sausages, bacon, scrambled eggs with smoked salmon, cereal, toast, muffins, pancakes, fruit, yogurt. Dylan eyed them all. Her appetite, which had waned after her meeting with Dr Starling, had returned. In fact, it seemed stronger than ever since she had trumped Lynsey at the mall in front of Nat and his friends.

When she finally finished piling up her plate, Dylan joined Honey and Lynsey at a table by the far windows. It looked out over a grassy slope that ran down to the library and art studios.

"You didn't need to bring breakfast for all three of us," Lynsey remarked, eyeing Dylan's tray. "We've already got ours."

Dylan stared back at Lynsey's tray in amazement. All she had was a bowl of cereal and a small plate of fruit. Dylan thought this was another strike against Lynsey. Who could trust someone who selected cereal and dried fruit when there was a full buffet?

"Prunes?" Dylan asked, trying not to grin.

"Dates," Lynsey snapped.

"So," Honey said, "are you going to see Morello today?"

"Of course," Dylan said enthusiastically. "Just as soon as I make my way through this. It's not often that I get a bigger breakfast than the horses! Anyway, I thought I'd smuggle Morello an apple. I've got to stay on his good side with the tryouts so soon. I'm only going to have a few practices before the big day." She looked at Lynsey, but her roommate did not respond with a tailor-made retort. She just stirred the leftover flakes of Special K around in her bowl.

Dylan scooped up a forkful of eggs. As far as she was concerned, she didn't need to hold any ill will against Lynsey. She felt she had let Lynsey know what she thought of her role in her detention, so they were on even ground again. Lynsey, however, seemed to be brewing a long-standing grudge.

Dylan saw Malory leave the cafeteria, and she swallowed her last mouthful of coffee before hurrying after her. They hadn't talked in over a week, and Dylan knew Malory probably wanted to keep it that way.

"Hey, Mal, wait up!" she called. She wasn't sure if Malory had heard her. Malory kept on walking down the hallway at the same even pace, and Dylan had to run to catch her.

"Mal!" she called out again as she grabbed her arm. "Didn't you hear me?"

Malory pulled her arm out of Dylan's grasp. "Yes. But I didn't think you'd say anything I wanted to hear."

Dylan flinched a little, but knew she deserved it. "Look, I just wanted to say I'm sorry for accusing you of calling Ali. I know it wasn't you."

Malory stared at her for a moment. "There's a surprise. So who was it?"

"I don't know for sure," Dylan admitted. "But I have a pretty good idea. Anyway, I shouldn't have blamed you."

Malory's face darkened. "You know, if you'd apologized before finding out it wasn't me, I'd have listened. But the only reason you're saying sorry is because you think you've found out that someone else turned you in. That doesn't matter to me. I just can't believe you thought that I would have done something like that. What did I ever to do you?"

Dylan's mouth dropped open. She couldn't think of a single thing to say, because she knew that Malory was absolutely right. They had disagreed over the whole Emily and Morello mess, but that felt like nothing now.

"You're just a typical Chestnut Hill girl, Dylan,"

Malory went on, her voice trembling. "Always thinking that you're better than everyone else, thinking you deserve to be an exception."

"Hey!" Dylan protested feebly.

"Truth hurts, huh?" Malory said before turning away. As she pushed past Dylan, she murmured, "And I thought you might be different."

Dylan stood still and watched Malory head down the hallway, too stunned to try and call her back. She realized the repercussions of truth-or-dare would not be over by the end of her ban. She might never earn back Malory's trust.

"No, no, no! A violin should be played with feeling. You are dragging the bow across the strings as if you're waging a war!" Mr Highland tapped his baton on Dylan's music stand. "Start again, and this time, think about the emotion in the music."

The emotion in the music? What about the emotion in me? Dylan thought. Usually she enjoyed her private violin lessons – her mother had forced her to pursue something "cultural" and had been ecstatic when Dylan had actually shown some skill. But today the clock hands seemed to be moving in slow motion. It was Monday, the first day she was allowed back in the saddle. As far as Dylan was concerned, every minute away from the stable was a minute wasted.

How could she concentrate on a Schubert waltz when her heart was racing to the *William Tell Overture*? She'd missed Morello like crazy right from the start, but she was now more anxious than ever to ride her best at the tryouts. She and Morello had something to prove – to Lynsey and everyone else. To misquote Mr Highland, this wasn't just a feeling – it was war! She glanced at her watch for the hundredth time. Just another five minutes until she could grab a sandwich and head down to the yard.

"Ms Carmichael," Dylan called to her aunt, who was crossing the yard carrying a grooming kit. "Would it be OK if I groom Morello for this afternoon's lesson?"

"What about your lunch?"

"I already had it," Dylan said, thinking of the half-eaten cheese sandwich that she'd tossed in the trash on the way down to the yard. "I'd just like to spend some extra time with Morello before riding him – you know, bond with him again?"

"I don't think there's much chance he's forgotten you!" Ali Carmichael smiled. "I think he's as keyed up for your return as you are. Go on," she said. "I'm pretty sure Kelly hasn't gotten the chance to groom him yet."

"Sounds good," Dylan said. "Thanks, Ms Carmichael." Before her aunt could respond, she darted toward the barn. She couldn't wait to get a body brush in her hand and start working it over the paint's satiny coat. She might not have any best friends in her class, but at least she had Morello.

"Come on, Dylan!" Lani was waiting outside the barn on Colorado. She gave her the thumbs up as Dylan led

Morello onto the yard. Dylan had been a little concerned that Lani might have turned against her. She had no idea whether Malory would have told her roommate about their latest argument. But Lani seemed as open and supportive as ever.

While being back in the yard felt like second nature, Dylan had to hop twice before she managed to swing herself up over Morello's back. "Argh." She made a face as the muscles in her thighs protested. "You'd think it was two months since I last did this, not just two weeks."

Lani leaned down to check Colorado's girth. "You're going to be sore tomorrow, that's for sure."

"Thanks for reminding me," Dylan said. "Are there any other words of encouragement you want to share before I head down to the arena?"

"Yeah, eat my dust!" Lani whooped, squeezing Colorado into a trot. His hooves clattered loudly as he passed Morello.

Dylan laughed as she felt Morello pull forward. "It's great to be back," she told the paint gelding, shortening her reins as he followed Colorado.

Down in the ring, Ali Carmichael already had the rest of the group working without their stirrups. "Drop your irons and fall in at the end of the line," she told Dylan and Lani. Dylan crossed her stirrups over Morello's neck, then waited for the group to ride by before joining them.

"Nice to have you back, Dylan," Honey called as she bounced past on Kingfisher. Even though she was one of the smallest seventh-graders, she had the long-legged gelding working really well, with his nose tucked in and his quarters under him. Dylan could tell his gait was a bit rough for a sitting trot, but Honey made it look easy. Dylan felt a warm glow at how good it felt to be back with the group, even if Lynsey and Malory trotted by without sparing her a glance.

She spent the warm-up session concentrating harder than she ever had before. She was determined to give herself every chance of turning in a great performance on Saturday. It was as if Morello was rooting for her. He didn't put a foot wrong, and Dylan felt a thrill as he bent around her leg on the corner with his neck arched at the canter.

"Excellent job, everyone," Ali Carmichael said. "Take your stirrups back and ride down to the other end of the arena. Except you, Malory."

Knowing they were done on the flat and moving on to fences, Dylan felt her stomach flip with a mixture of nerves and excitement. She leaned forward to pat Morello's warm neck as Malory cantered a circle around the course of jumps, admiring the quiet way she was able to get the very best out of Hardy. When he laid back his ears halfway through the course and tried to swerve back to the other horses, Malory already had her outside leg pressed against his side and her inside rein shortened to redirect him.

Hardy was a careful jumper who needed his rider to give him encouragement while still keeping him balanced, because he tended to use speed instead of power to get over the fences. Dylan noticed that Malory held him in check between every jump but still gave him plenty of impulsion with her legs and seat. She never let the chestnut cob feel he was jumping by himself for one second, and she made him look like a winner.

It struck Dylan that she never saw Malory so relaxed as when she was riding. *It's like she's more at home when she's with the horses*, Dylan thought. There was so much she admired about Malory. *But I blew it*, she figured ruefully as Malory approached the final combination. She couldn't think of anything to say that wouldn't sound like she was trying to suck up to Malory after their argument. Instead, she dropped her reins and clapped hard when the pair sailed over the final fence.

Malory shot her a startled glance as she cantered past, making way for Lynsey on Bluegrass. But Dylan noticed that her cheeks flushed pink when the rest of the group took up the applause.

Bluegrass went over each jump easily, and Lynsey stroked his neck just once with her immaculate white-gloved hand as they finished. Dylan noticed that even though they had a clear round, the applause wasn't as loud as it had been for Malory, and she wondered if anyone else suspected that Lynsey had told on her. Not that it made any difference, since Dylan was trying to move past that whole mess anyway.

As Bluegrass returned to the group, Dylan marvelled at the pony's perfection. He didn't even pin his ears or bite at flies. Dylan smiled and flicked some of Morello's mane over his neck so it was lying on the right side. *Give me a real horse any day*, she thought, gathering her reins as her aunt nodded for her to ride next.

It was as if the two-week ban had never happened. Dylan felt that she and Morello were totally in sync as they took the first jump. When they thudded down on the other side, the gelding snatched at the bit, making it jangle. Dylan quickly gave and took with the reins to get his concentration back on the fences. "Good boy," she murmured, and he lowered his head and flickered back his ear to show he was listening to her.

She was almost convinced they were going to make a clear round as they approached the last fence, but she leaned forward a stride too soon and broke Morello's concentration. Morello rattled the last part of the combination with his back hooves, and Dylan looked around to see the pole bobble in its cup holders and then fall with a thud onto the sand. "Never mind, boy," she leaned forward to pull gently at one of Morello's ears. "That was wonderful!"

She grinned at Lani, who shouted, "Yay, Walsh!" Picking up on Dylan's high spirits, Morello snatched at the reins and gave a playful buck. Dylan had to trot two circles before she could persuade the gelding that they were done.

Bring on the tryouts, she thought, crossing her fingers. She and Morello were back on track, and she knew that, together, they had a shot at getting on the team.

Chapter Twelve

It was Friday, the day before the tryouts, and none of the seventh-grade intermediate riders had been able to concentrate during art class.

It had been that way all week for Dylan. Every hour felt like five, unless she was in the stable or actually riding. That time raced by, and she had to pray that she was making the most of it, practising the very things that would come into play on Saturday. Dylan worried that she and Morello still struggled with combination jumps and had little experience with the timed rounds, which would be important if they managed to get into the deciding jump-off. But, first things first. For now, Dylan was supposed to be painting a tree.

Paintbrush in hand, she stood back from the giant wall mural, which was based on an aerial shot of Chestnut Hill. Each girl was responsible for painting her own square. Dylan looked over and smiled at Lani, who had the tip of her tongue sticking out of her mouth as she dabbed at a detail on the fields around the school campus.

"Um, Lani, since when do cows have bushy tails?"

Lani leaned closer to her picture and let out a dramatic groan. "I've just painted Colorado's tail on a cow! I've got horses on the brain. When was this picture taken, anyway?" she asked. "We don't have any cows on campus now, do we?"

Dylan was trying to come up with a good response, but Honey spoke first.

"Don't worry, it can be painted out. Maybe you should let it dry a little and then go over it with green."

Lani's shoulders drooped, but then the bell sounded and the room exploded with activity as the girls hurried to clean their brushes and pack away their supplies. All of the intermediate riders had planned to go down to the yard during recess. There were no riding classes so the horses save their energy for the demanding workouts of the next day, but the girls didn't care. They all wanted as much last-minute bonding time as possible.

"Quietly, please," Mr Woolley said, walking around with a jar for the girls to put brushes in. As usual, his button-down shirt had almost as much paint on it as the mural. Even his loafers had dried multicoloured blobs all over them. Dylan absentmindedly plunked her brush in the container and took off her smock.

"Are you going to grab a snack before we go down to the stable?" Lani raised her voice over the noise of taps running.

"Yeah, as long as it's fast!" Dylan said, putting her paint tray on the drying rack. Then she grabbed her books and waved to Honey and Lani as she headed out the door.

Dylan headed across campus with her fingers crossed. Lynsey hadn't said a thing about the fact that she had not yet returned her shirt, and Dylan could only hope that was a good sign. Dylan had gone to the laundry room and requested specialist cleaning for the shirt, along with her best tan breeches for the tryouts. But when she pulled the T-shirt out of the netted bag, her heart sank. The chocolate ice cream had left a faint but obvious mark down the pale oyster silk.

Dylan tried to compose an acceptable excuse as she hurried across the lawn, dodging groups of girls trying to soak up the last of the afternoon's sun. As she ran up the steps that led to Adams, she swore she could smell the chocolate chip cookies that would be waiting for her. She contemplated taking the laundry back to her room, but the aroma was too tempting. *Well, I might as well get this over with*, she thought, anticipating a showdown with Lynsey.

The lounge was full of noise when Dylan pushed open the door. Her class had claimed their usual sofas by the window. Dylan dropped her laundry bag just inside the door and headed over to claim her share of the cookies.

"Hurry up. We're all ready to go down to the yard." Honey handed her a soda while Lani held out a plate of chocolate chip cookies.

Dylan offered a tentative smile, fully aware that Lynsey was right behind her. She headed over to her laundry bag and gingerly lifted the damaged garment.

"I had your top dry-cleaned," she said, handing it over. "I'm really sorry, but there was a stain that wouldn't come out."

"What stain?" Lynsey interrogated, grabbing the top and turning it over in her hands.

"I had a close encounter with a chocolate ice-cream cone," Dylan said apologetically. "I'll get you another one."

"Sure, the next time you're in Milan," Lynsey growled. She wadded up the T-shirt and threw it toward the wastepaper basket in the corner of the room.

"Oops, you missed," Lani said, breaking the stunned silence.

Lynsey ignored her. "I guess some people find it easy being careless with other people's property." She glanced knowingly at Patience, who was sitting alongside her.

Dylan's mouth dropped open. Was Lynsey trying to make a connection between her T-shirt and Dylan's riding Morello at night? "Well, we all know that I haven't been very careful recently. Like choosing who to trust, for a start. You practically forced me to borrow the shirt."

"I thought we were going down to the stables?" Malory stood up and put her drink down on the table. "Come on, Lynsey, it's just a T-shirt."

"It's not *just* a T-shirt," Lynsey retorted. "It's a Versace that my dad bought for me."

"What's the big deal about a label?" Malory asked back, picking her jacket off the floor. "Don't you have enough already? Can't you just have your dad call someone to get you a new one?"

Lynsey's jaw jutted out, and she put one hand on her hip. The room seemed to shift slightly as everyone took a breath to prepare for Lynsey's response. "What are you getting at, Malory?" It was more of an accusation than a question, and it sounded like Lynsey was just getting started. "Maybe I could ask my dad to call someone and order a new shirt, but you're one to talk. You're the one who used your connections to get the Rockwell Award. Everyone knows that's the only way you could have landed it."

Dylan wasn't sure what Lynsey was suggesting, but it seemed to have had an effect on Malory. All of the colour had drained out of her cheeks. "And just what is that supposed to mean?"

"Come off it. You don't own a horse, and you don't ride the decent show circuits. How else would you manage to win that grant?"

"That's what you think?" Malory spoke slowly.

"Yeah, I do," Lynsey snapped.

"Well, that's pretty funny," Malory said. "Because it just proves that you only think about yourself, your possessions, and the fact that you didn't get the precious Rockwell Award even though you're way more qualified. I wish you had gotten it, because then there is no way that I would be here right now." She looked around the room and took a breath.

Dylan thought she would turn around and leave, but she started talking again, staring at her hands.

"I have never felt so alone as I do here." Malory's voice faltered with each word. "And the funny thing is, I knew it would be like this. I had heard what Chestnut Hill girls were like, and I never wanted to be one."

Lynsey let out an exaggerated sigh, making Malory look up.

"I didn't get the scholarship because my dad bought it for me, if that's what you're all thinking," she hissed. "It's not like he'd be able to afford it, working at a shoe store."

"Your dad works at a *shoe store*!" Lynsey spoke the words like they were contaminated. "You've gotta be kidding me! There's no way they'd let anyone from a family like that into Chestnut Hill. How did you think you were going to fit in?"

"I didn't." Malory's eyes were bright and her voice shook, but she looked Lynsey straight in the eyes. "I knew I wouldn't, and I didn't even want to try. I'm only here because my dad made me come."

"Yeah, go tell that to someone who believes it." Lynsey rolled her eyes. "I know about girls like you. You'd give your last pair of Steve Madden mary janes to come to a place like this." She glanced down at her cherry-shimmer fingernails and shrugged. "Your dad does sell Steve Madden, doesn't he? Hmmmm, maybe not."

"I don't care what you believe!" Malory yelled. "My dad insisted this school was such a great opportunity." She glared at them and Dylan flinched. "I can't believe he was actually proud of me for getting the scholarship!"

"Why? Wasn't the local high school good enough for him?" Patience said.

"It suited us just fine…" Malory stopped.

"Until what? Why'd you come here?" Lynsey asked, raising an eyebrow.

"I came," Malory said flatly, "because my mother died. My dad thought I'd be better off here than at home. He was working all the time trying to pay the hospital bills. And the truth is, part of me did want to come here – for him. I wanted to be able to make him proud. He wanted me to have the chance to make something of myself."

She looked around, and Dylan felt herself drop her gaze in order to avoid the defiance burning in those blue eyes. "I wonder what he'd think if he could see me here now – with all of you," Malory finished quietly. Keeping her head high, she turned and walked out of the room.

There was a stunned silence in the room. Slowly, the girls looked around, trying to assess the damage. Lani was the first to speak. "Way to go, Lynsey."

"Don't blame her," Patience insisted. "It was Dylan who started the whole thing by ruining Lynsey's shirt."

"Did any of you guys know about her mom?" Alexandra asked in a hushed voice.

"How could we?" Wei Lin said in a guilt-ridden tone. "The girl hardly ever talked."

"It was news to me," Lynsey stated, glancing around the room. But Dylan noticed that none of the other girls would meet her eyes. Lynsey turned to Patience. "I'm going to see Blue – are you coming?"

The room fell silent as Lynsey and Patience gathered their things and left.

"Wow," Dylan breathed. Even the upperclassmen on the other side of the room were staring at them. "We sure know how to keep things exciting around here."

"Should we go after Malory?" Razina asked, her brown eyes troubled.

Lani looked thoughtful. "Maybe she needs some time on her own."

"Yeah," Alexandra agreed. "It couldn't have been easy having all her personal stuff hit the fan in front of everyone. I mean, she's always been a bit secretive, but I guess she had her reasons. I can't believe Lynsey would drag all that stuff out of her like that."

Honey broke off a piece of cookie with one hand. "I think everyone seems the same when they arrive at boarding school. We go through all the same day-to-day stuff together, but who knows what's going on under the surface?"

Razina nodded. "Totally. And it looks like Malory has had a lot more to deal with than the rest of us. It was probably just a matter of time before she'd need to confess it to someone."

"Yeah," Lani agreed. "But I'm guessing the last person she would have chosen was Lynsey."

Dylan didn't say anything. She was wondering if Malory had headed to the stables. That's where she would have gone if things had blown up like that. She was frustrated that she hadn't been able to be a friend to Malory. She had been suspicious of her secrecy, and, apparently, so had everyone else. And now that Malory needed a friend, there wasn't anyone who could comfort her.

When Malory didn't show up for dinner, Dylan became concerned. "I'm going to see if I can find her," she announced, pushing away her uneaten dinner. She got up from the table and headed for the door.

"Wait up!" Dylan looked over her shoulder and saw Lani and Honey hurrying to catch up with her.

"We'll come with you," Lani offered. "I can't eat, either, which is saying something when it's quesadillas. I really love Monterey Jack!" Dylan gave Lani a sideways glance as she pushed open the dining hall door.

"Where do you think she'll be?" Honey asked, out of breath.

Dylan shrugged. "The most obvious place is in the barn, with Hardy."

Honey glanced at her watch. "For all this time?"

"It's worth a shot, isn't it?" Dylan said. The longer Malory stayed away, the worse it made her feel. It hardly seemed possible that the whole thing started when Malory had tried to stick up for Dylan when she confessed about ruining the T-shirt. *I'm never wearing Versace again*, she vowed.

The girls walked down to the barn in the fading light without talking. It was almost seven o'clock, and although there were a few girls hurrying toward the athletic centre, the rest of the campus was quiet.

As they entered the stable, Dylan strode ahead, almost running down the aisle to Hardy's stall. She was sure she'd find Malory curled up in the back corner. But when she peered over the door, only Hardy was there, pulling at his hay. He looked at Dylan with his ears pricked hopefully.

"Sorry, boy. I don't have anything for you," she apologized, showing her empty hands.

"Any luck?" Honey called.

"No." Dylan shook her head bleakly. "What do we do now?"

"You don't really think she could have run away, do you? Maybe we should let Mrs Herson know," Honey said as they walked back to Adams House after searching the rest of the campus.

"I think we should give her a while longer," Dylan said. The last thing she wanted was to get Malory in trouble. *This semester has been hard enough for her. She doesn't need to have a record for truancy, too.*

"How about we check the dorm rooms again before we decide what to do next?" Lani suggested.

"We could get the others to help. Eight of us

covering the dorm has got to be better than three," Honey pointed out.

"That's a great idea," Dylan said. "She's got to be somewhere close by." But remembering the expression on Malory's face earlier, Dylan wouldn't have blamed her if she had gone as far as she could.

Lani led the way up to the room that she shared with Malory and Alexandra. Honey squeezed Dylan's arm as Lani pushed open the door and stepped inside the room. Lani let out an exclamation. Dylan and Honey looked at one another in alarm and hurried into the room in time to hear Lani say, "Hey, where've you been hiding? We missed you at dinner tonight."

"I went for a walk, and I wasn't hungry so I decided to skip dinner." Malory was sitting cross-legged on her bed, polishing her riding boots.

She must have walked around the campus six times! Dylan thought, thinking how long she'd been gone. They hadn't seen her for hours, but Malory still looked the same – drained and disheartened.

"We thought you might have been down with Hardy," Lani told her, sitting beside Malory on her bed.

"We were really worried about you," Dylan added.

Malory gave a short, humourless laugh. "Sure you were."

Dylan felt her cheeks burn. "Mal," she started awkwardly.

"Look, we've all got a busy day tomorrow, and I'd really appreciate it if you would leave me alone so I can get some sleep," Malory said without looking up.

Dylan felt like she had a lot more to say to Malory. And even though she didn't know where to start, she didn't want to leave.

Honey tugged gently on her arm. "Come on," she said. "Malory's right. We all need some sleep, and maybe things will look better in the morning."

But as Dylan followed Honey from the room, she had a gut feeling that, come the light of day, things wouldn't be any better at all.

Chapter Thirteen

Dylan's fingers fumbled as she tried to button up her riding shirt. She couldn't remember the last time she had been this nervous – not even before the state finals at the end of the summer. Honey and Lynsey had already left for the stable, but Dylan was running late. She hadn't been able to find her boots, completely forgetting that she had put them outside the door the night before.

Just as she finished tying her laces, Lani appeared at the threshold of the room.

"Oh, great!" Dylan exclaimed, "We can go down together."

But Lani just stood there with a shocked expression. "It's Malory," she burst out, her cheeks flushed. "She's packing. She's leaving Chestnut Hill!"

"What?" Dylan jumped off the bed and rushed for the door.

"I've tried everything to make her stay," Lani said as they raced down the hallway. "I even promised to stop singing Celine Dion songs in the shower! But she's determined to leave. She says she has nothing to offer Chestnut Hill and it has nothing to offer her. I tried telling her that she's got more talent in her little finger than Lynsey has in her entire body and that her dad would want her to stay, but she just isn't listening."

"What makes you think I can stop her?" Dylan asked as they neared the room.

Lani stopped outside her room and shrugged. "Everyone else has already gone down for the tryouts. You were the only one here."

"Thanks," Dylan said.

"I'm just kidding. But I really don't know. You like to pick fights, right? Here's your chance. Just do your best, OK?"

Dylan nodded, although she didn't have a clue where to start. If anyone deserved to be at Chestnut Hill, it was Malory. She had proven that. "Go down to the stable," Dylan said to Lani. "There's no point in both of us being late for tryouts."

"OK, if you're sure," Lani said, watching as Dylan stepped into the room.

Malory looked up from folding a pair of jeans. Two suitcases were open on the bed, both half full of clothes. "You won't change my mind, so why don't you close the door on your way out?" she said bluntly, turning to place the jeans in one of the cases.

"Come on, Mal," Dylan began. "You know that no

one wants you to leave." But she had to admit that her words didn't sound very convincing.

"Really?" Malory snapped, turning back around. "I bet when Lynsey finds out, she'll throw a party."

Dylan's lips twitched. "Maybe. But I bet it will be black-tie with a limited guest list."

Malory clearly wasn't in the mood for Dylan's sense of humour. "Look, you should leave. You'll miss the tryouts."

Dylan glanced at the clock on the wall and saw that they were both cutting it close. Her own tryout slot was in less than thirty minutes, and Malory's might even be before that. Her heart skipped a beat, but as she looked at Malory, she remembered how she had tricked Nutmeg that first day, crawling on the ground, and somehow Dylan knew she couldn't leave yet.

But the question was, how would she convince Malory to stay? After all, Dylan was part of the reason Malory wanted to go. Malory had been frustrated with her for valuing Morello's safety over Emily's. Then Dylan had wrongly accused Malory of turning her in to the administration. Dylan had done just what Malory expected of a Chestnut Hill girl – put her own interests first, no matter the cost. But now it was in Dylan's interest to change Malory's mind. She wanted her to stay, and she wanted to know her better. And she really wanted Malory to teach her tricks like the one she used on Nutmeg.

"So this is it?" Dylan asked before she realized what she was saying. "You're going to take the easy way out?

It's not really what I had expected from you."

"What?" Malory looked up from what she was doing, obviously thrown.

Dylan shrugged. "I didn't think you were a quitter. I thought you were stronger than that. But I guess even I can't be right all of the time."

Malory's mouth dropped open. "You've got a lot of nerve."

Dylan crossed her arms. "You know you don't really want to leave," she said.

"Oh, yes, I do."

"No, you don't," Dylan said with more conviction this time. "If you did, you wouldn't be carefully folding all of your clothes into your suitcases – you'd be stuffing them in. Anything to get out of here as fast as possible."

Malory's hands clenched into fists at her side. "First of all, Dylan Walsh, you don't know me. And secondly–"

Dylan raised her eyebrows.

"You don't know me," Malory snapped again, turning around to empty another drawer of clothes. She banged it shut with her foot.

"You know something, you're right," Dylan confessed. "I don't know you. I had you down as the most together girl here. Sure, it bugged me the way you never opened up about anything and I didn't get why you always wanted to clean tack instead of hanging out–"

"Not that it's anything to you," Malory interrupted

in a huff, "but I didn't play truth-or-dare because I didn't want to do anything that would make me lose the scholarship."

Dylan realized her argument had gotten off track. "I don't care about that now. It's fine if you don't want everyone knowing about your personal life."

"I think it's a little late for that." Malory dropped a pair of socks on the floor but didn't seem to notice. "Great, fine, whatever. If you're so big on privacy, why don't you just leave me alone?"

"Well, I could. But, as a last favour, I'll help you pack." Malory looked at Dylan but didn't say anything. "Because if you really think that you have nothing to give Chestnut Hill and Chestnut Hill has nothing to give you, then maybe you *should* leave." Dylan bent down to pick up the socks and tossed them into the case. "It's probably for the best. I mean, why should anyone rival the Lynsey Harrisons of the world? They know that talent doesn't really matter – it's all about how much money you pour into equitation classes. There's no way you have anything worthwhile to teach the classic Chestnut Hill girl. I know I have nothing to learn from you – not in life and especially not anything to do with horses. You're really just wasting our time if you don't have any clothes we can borrow." Dylan stopped, not knowing if she was getting anywhere. She had a bad feeling she was just proving Malory's point.

Malory reached into her closet and grabbed a bunch of shirts still on their hangers, but she looked back at Dylan expectantly.

"Where do you want your riding stuff?" Dylan asked, pulling out a dresser drawer.

"Anywhere," Malory said.

Dylan started pulling stuff from the drawer and putting it in the closest suitcase. "You know, I'm glad you're going," she added. "Because now I don't have to feel bad about accusing you of telling on me. I mean, we wouldn't have been friends anyway, so no loss, right?" She bent down and lifted up a pile of jodhpurs. "And, Malory, I have to say that the real winners in this are the horses. I'm sure Hardy will be glad to see you gone. He probably wants to be ridden by someone who competes in all the top shows. A real Chestnut Hill girl who thinks she can buy ribbons. Someone like that would really get the best out of him – might even make the competition team."

"Oh, we would have made the team," Malory declared. Dylan recognized a defiant tone in her voice. "What are you doing with my jodhpurs?" Malory asked suddenly.

"Packing them."

"Hand them over," Malory said, reaching out her hand. "We both know Hardy deserves to be on that team."

Dylan looked at Malory. Her eyes looked soft with tears but her jaw was determined. "Really? Are you sure?" Dylan asked.

"Don't ask me that. I might change my mind," Malory threatened. She tipped her head to the side and gave Dylan the first genuine smile she'd seen. "OK, you convinced me, I do have something to offer Chestnut Hill. And maybe there are some things about this place that aren't so bad. I actually like some of the horses."

"Oh, stop your gushing and hurry up," Dylan said, throwing a pair of riding trousers at Malory and rummaging through her luggage in search of a shirt and jacket. She felt something start to swell inside her, and she recognized it as hope. "Quick, put on your show clothes. There's no way we can miss tryouts now!"

Malory and Dylan ran across the lawn toward the indoor arena. The air was clear and crisp, but the sun was bold – an exquisite day for riding. Horses were tied along the outside wall of the barn, their tails swishing as they waited their turn. Everywhere Dylan looked, girls dressed in dark coats and pristine breeches were dashing around with sponges, buckets of water, and armfuls of clean, well-conditioned tack. Dylan could practically smell the saddle soap.

"There's Lani with Hardy!" she panted.

The moment Lani saw them, she slipped off the halter that had been buckled over Hardy's bridle and led him over. A cheer burst from the indoor arena as Joy Richards rode out. Her pony's flanks were flecked with foam and, instead of tying him up when she dismounted, she led him to the far end of the yard to walk him in circles so that he could cool down.

Like clockwork, Kathryn MacIntyre from Meyer was announced and she disappeared into the indoor arena on Snapdragon, a dapple-grey pony.

"Not a second to spare." Lani grinned at Malory. "I tacked him up in case you changed your mind."

"Well, I did," Malory smiled, tightening her chin strap.

"You'd better get on – you're next," Lani told her. She looked across at Dylan. "Morello's waiting for you in the barn, cooling off after his last round. I checked on him a few minutes ago."

"Thanks, Lani. We both owe you," Dylan said, holding Hardy's stirrup so Malory could mount.

Malory swung into the saddle and then glanced down at her. "If I don't see you again before you ride, good luck. Remember not to get ahead of him and you'll do great."

The girls looked up to see Kathryn ride back out of the arena. She looked disappointed. "Watch out for the final combination," she called to Malory. "You just have to look at the top pole for it to fall off."

Malory glanced up from checking her girth and gave a nervous smile. She and Hardy hadn't even had time for a practice fence.

"You heard the girl. Ride it with your eyes closed and you'll be fine." Lani gave Hardy's quarters a gentle slap as Malory squeezed him forward.

"Good luck," Lani and Dylan called at the same time, watching Malory and Hardy disappear through the doors. Dylan felt all her hopes go with them until Lani snapped her fingers in front of Dylan's face.

"OK, Dyl. Emily Page had the final fence down on her round with Morello," Lani told her. "In fact, she had the second and fifth fences down, too, so she's almost definitely out of it. Morello seemed kind of nervous with her."

Dylan nodded. "I'm going to go get him now. I'm up just one after Malory."

She jogged a few strides toward the barn and then paused. "Wait! How did you do?" With the distraction of getting Malory into the ring, she'd totally forgotten that Lani had ridden earlier.

"We scraped by with a clear, " Lani told her with a smile. "I bribed Colorado with my mom's homemade apple pie. All that sugar really helps him focus."

"Congrats!" Dylan said, with a little clap.

"Thanks," Lani smiled. "Oh, and Honey got eight faults – she ran into some grief on the combination. Lynsey – surprise, surprise – went clear, and quite a few of the eighth-graders had clear rounds, too."

"So the competition's stiff," Dylan called over her shoulder as she set off again.

"Nothing you can't handle, Walsh," Lani's voice rang out after her.

Listening to her footsteps echo down the barn's central aisle, Dylan wasn't so sure. She'd had a surefire plan to make certain that Morello was ready for their round – a plan that had included several practice fences and some solid bonding time. Persuading Malory not to take off was the last thing she had expected, but Dylan didn't really care if it had blown her chances of winning a spot on the junior jumping team. Malory was staying, and that fact made Dylan feel as if she'd already won.

Chapter Fourteen

When she rode through the double doors to the indoor arena, Dylan gulped at the sea of faces lining the bleachers. She took a deep breath and tore her eyes away from the seating gallery. The only thing that mattered for the next minute and a half was the course of eight fences that she and Morello needed to jump clear if she wanted a chance of making the junior team. There was little consolation in the fact that Morello had already seen the course with Emily Page. Based on Lani's report of their faults, his earlier round could prove to be a psychological disadvantage. Dylan had to ride with enough confidence to overcome Morello's past missteps.

Dylan gave the gelding a quick scratch on the neck. "It's you and me this time, boy," she murmured. "We can do this."

His ears flicked back at the sound of her voice, and, from the bounce in his step, Dylan knew that he was just waiting for her to tell him what to do next. She pushed him into a steady canter and circled once before heading for the first fence. On her way past the door, she caught a glimpse of Malory standing in the gap.

Remember not to get ahead of him. Malory's advice echoed in her mind. Dylan knew Malory was right. It was all about rhythm. If she and Morello were together at every fence, they had a good shot. Dylan tried to see all of the fences through Morello's eyes, holding him in until the last moment on some, urging him forward on others. Morello responded each time, adjusting his pace just as she asked. Dylan knew he needed to have his hocks right under him to spring over the uprights but more speed to clear the spreads. When they approached the final combination, Dylan wasn't even sure how they had done. All her concentration had been in getting over one jump and then preparing Morello for the next. She hadn't even thought to listen for any falling poles.

Her heart began to pound uncomfortably at the sight of the final dreaded obstacle. It was a classic in-and-out, with two fences paced just a stride apart. But now Dylan saw that the two red-and-white jumps were placed incredibly close, which was why the second one kept falling. The takeoff was incredibly tight. Picking up on her hesitancy, Morello faltered in his stride.

"Sorry, boy. I'm with you all the way," she whispered.

Morello recovered quickly, and with his ears pricked forward, he cleared the first fence, put in one short stride, and sailed over the second. Dylan sat quietly until they landed on the soft sand. She didn't look back at the jumps to see if any poles were lying on the ground. All she could hear was the thudding of Morello's hooves as she slowed him from a canter to a steady, bouncing trot.

It was only when the arena filled with the sound of clapping that she dared to believe that they had actually scored the clear round they needed.

"Nice work," Ali Carmichael announced as she joined Dylan just outside the arena. She spoke briskly, glancing down at her red clipboard. "I didn't see you earlier, so I'll give you the full rundown on the jump-off. You're going to have to ride against everyone who went clear. That's Lynsey, Lani, and Malory from your group, and Eleanor Dixon, Aster Sachs-Cohen, Olivia Buckley, Victoria Rasmussen, and Joy Richards," she said. "This round is timed. You're fifth in line, so you'll have a chance to develop strategy." Ali shrugged off her yard coat and slung it over her shoulder before looking her niece in the eye. "You rode Morello better than ever. Just make sure you do it a second time."

"I'll do my best," Dylan promised, slipping off Morello and loosening his girth. When she looked up, her aunt was already hurrying away, calling out the riding order to the other girls who had a clear first round. Most of their ponies were tied to rings along the barn wall so they could rest while still tacked up. Sarah and Kelly were busy filling buckets of water at the outdoor tap, preparing to sponge the ponies down later.

Dylan caught Malory's eye as her friend swung

herself up onto Hardy. She was riding second, after Lynsey. "I'd wish you luck, but I don't think you need it."

Malory smiled. "Everyone can use a little luck, so thanks. I'll be pulling for you, too."

Dylan let Malory's words sink in and realized how much they meant to her. She wondered if it was really possible that they would become friends after all they'd been through. But her thoughts didn't linger there long; she needed to focus on her timed round. She just wanted to get back into the ring so Morello could prove how talented he was again.

With a clatter of hooves, Lynsey rode past on Bluegrass without even acknowledging Dylan. Her back was stiff, and Bluegrass tossed his head in protest over her tight hold on the reins. Dylan felt a jab of sympathy for her. Even though Lynsey had a top-class pedigree in competitions, none of that mattered today. Everyone had an equal chance, and it was obvious that the pressure was getting to her. *It must be difficult to have a reputation to live up to*, Dylan thought, watching her disappear into the arena.

Morello stamped his foot impatiently, and Dylan decided to walk him toward the paddocks to calm both of their nerves. She rested her arm over his neck and thought through the next course. The fences were in the same order, but they would be a few inches higher, which would affect the pacing. And she needed to figure out where she could shave off time. It seemed like only seconds before she heard the loudspeaker crackle to announce that Lynsey had pulled off another clear round in one minute, eighteen seconds. *As to be expected*, Dylan thought. Dylan led Morello to the end of the fence and turned around when the loudspeaker came to life again.

"Malory O'Neil on Hardy-Har-Har, zero faults, one minute and twenty seconds."

Dylan let out a whoop of celebration and quickened her pace back to the collecting area. She waved as soon as she saw Malory. "Congrats!"

"One minute twenty!" Malory sighed with relief. "One more second and I would have picked up a time fault. I know I was on the slow side, but Hardy is such a careful jumper that I worried about pushing him for more speed."

"You totally deserve a place on the team. I'm sure you'll make it," Dylan said warmly. "You, too, Hardy-Har-Har." The pony's show name made her smile, and she gave the stocky gelding a pat.

Malory laughed. "We're not on it yet. Everyone else might ride a faster round than me."

As if to prove her wrong, Victoria Rasmussen rode out with two time faults. "And I knocked down the last fence," she said, slipping off Soda, who looked much bigger than his 15.3 hands against her tiny frame. "They changed that last in-and-out, so it's now a really long stride between the two." Dylan smiled sympathetically at the petite blond as she led Soda away, and then thought about how the change to the combination affected her.

"Do you think I can cut the corner heading into the spread?" she asked.

Malory frowned. "Yes, but don't make it too tight. He'll need to take off a little early to clear the width."

Just then there was a groan from inside the arena. One of the favorites to make the team, Aster Sachs-Cohen, who was riding on her own pony, Mermaid, rode out with six faults. Dylan felt a tug of disappointment; Aster was in Adams, and it would have been good for the dorm if she'd made the team.

"I took the whole thing too fast," Dylan overheard her say to Eleanor Dixon. "You need to watch out for the wall – it might look like you can take off two strides away from the corner, but you're better off with a short three!" Aster bit her lip as she patted Mermaid's neck. "It wasn't your fault, girl," she said.

Dylan's turn came around much faster than she had anticipated. Malory had tied Hardy to a ring so she could watch Dylan from inside. They walked together until they reached the arena doors. "You can do it," Malory called.

"Go, Walsh!" Over on the opposite side of the arena, Dylan saw Honey, Razina, and others from their floor, waving.

Dylan's mouth was dry as she shortened her reins and sent Morello forward. She looked up at the digital clock on the wall. It was set to zero. She knew that the moment she crossed the starting line, the seconds would start racing against her.

As Morello crossed the starting line toward the first fence, the buzzer went off. Morello kept his pace to the easy vertical. The moment he landed, Dylan closed her legs around him, telling him he needed to go faster than before. With a snort, Morello extended his stride to the second fence of the line, which was at the top of the ring. When they reached the corner, Dylan closed her hands on the reins, knowing they needed to keep their rhythm through the turn. Morello flicked back his ear and brought his quarters under him before clearing the wall easily. Next was the spread, and, instead of allowing Morello three strides after the wall, Dylan turned him after two to save time. She saw almost immediately that it was a mistake. The distance was too much for Morello to cover in two strides. She half-halted to make room for a third, but he was still too close. Morello pitched himself forward, jumping almost on top of the fence.

Sure enough, Dylan heard his hooves hit the top bar, but she was right with him. When he landed, she sat back and gave him leg. Morello lengthened his stride to come out OK on the other end of the combination, but Dylan knew she couldn't afford to knock anything else down. She glanced at the clock and saw that her pace put her a whole second in front of Lynsey. *If I don't pick up any other faults, I might still have a chance of making the team.* She steadied Morello and concentrated on the final three jumps, remembering she'd need some speed to make it through the long in-and-out.

Morello opened up his canter and flew over the final combination, and Dylan's heart raced with adrenaline. Then she heard a groan from the bleachers. Dylan glanced over her shoulder and saw the top pole of the final fence lying on the ground. Her stomach dropped. Knocking down two poles gave her eight faults, which would surely take her out of the running. She couldn't believe it. They had taken all the fences together, but it wasn't enough.

"Never mind, boy." She swallowed hard as she rode out of the ring, feeling mad at herself for trying to shave off time between the wall and the spread.

When Dylan rode out into the sunshine, Malory was waiting. "Way to go!" she cried. "One minute, ten seconds. No time faults."

Dylan bit her lip. "I knocked down two poles. That puts me behind Aster Sachs-Cohen."

Malory shook her head. "No, you didn't. You only knocked down the last fence. He bumped that spread, but the rail didn't fall. So you only got four faults. Didn't you listen to the loudspeaker?"

Dylan slipped off Morello. "Well, I guess four faults are better than eight, but there are four more riders to go, and someone's bound to go clear. I mean, I don't think Eleanor Dixon knows what it's like to bring down a fence. And Lani is an absolute speed demon."

As if to prove her point, a few moments later Eleanor Dixon trotted out of the arena, calling out, "Clear, one minute nine," to Joy Richards, who was waiting to go on Buttercup. Joy gave her girth one last check and then disappeared through the entrance on the palomino. *So that's Eleanor, Mal, and Lynsey all ahead of me. And it will be a walk in the park for Joy Richards, who made the team last year as a seventh-grader. It looks like the reserve place is going to be fought out between Lani, Olivia, and me*. Dylan glanced across at the two girls, who were quietly walking their ponies around the far end of the yard. Lani had disappeared after Dylan rode her first round, and she seemed unusually subdued now. Dylan thought it best not to disturb her.

Dylan heard clapping come from the arena, and Joy trotted out. "Good work," Dylan called, trying to swallow her own disappointment. Joy gave her a tight smile before slipping down to the ground.

"Are you trying to rub it in?" Malory whispered, giving Dylan's arm a nudge.

"Huh?"

Malory tightened her grip on Hardy's reins as he stamped his foot. "She had eight faults. That was consolation applause. You really have to pay attention to the announcements!" Malory shook her head in disbelief. "So there are still two slots left."

"And Olivia and Lani still have to go," Dylan pointed out.

"Dylan Walsh! You are a lousy pessimist," Malory exclaimed.

"I'll have you know I'm never pessimistic," Dylan said as Olivia trotted past on Shamrock. "I am, however, always realistic."

"Do you have an answer for everything?" Malory asked.

"Yes," Dylan assured her. "It's a gift." Despite her jittery stomach, she smiled.

Malory rolled her eyes, but Dylan was feeling

grateful for her company. Malory now knew that she was guaranteed a spot on the team, and, instead of celebrating, she was willing to wait it out until they knew Dylan's fate as well.

For the next few moments they stood in silence, stroking Morello and Hardy's noses as they waited for Olivia to finish. When she clattered out onto the yard on the bright bay mare, the loudspeaker announced, "Clear round, one minute nineteen." Dylan's heart began to pound. *She's in. It's down to Lani and me.* She couldn't believe her luck. Why did it have to be Lani, of all people?

At that moment, Dylan saw Lani ride by, looking straight ahead with a determined expression.

"Good luck," Dylan and Malory called. Of course Dylan wanted Lani to ride her best, but she couldn't help hoping that her best wasn't less than four faults. Malory grinned, as if she knew exactly how torn Dylan was feeling.

"I can't take this," Dylan said after a moment. "Will you hold Morello for me so I can go watch?"

"Sure," Malory agreed with a self-assured smirk. "I'll tighten up his girth as well – just in case you need to be riding back into the arena in a few minutes for a formal celebration."

As Dylan hurried to the entrance, she crossed her fingers, but she knew it was a long shot. When it came to racing the clock, Lani was the most amazing rider Dylan had ever seen. *Granted, her equitation leaves something to be desired*, Dylan thought, but Dylan knew that sitting up straight and keeping your heels down didn't matter here. It was all about speed and faults, and Lani had speed down. Even though Dylan had watched her carefully at every practice, she still couldn't figure out how Lani managed to shave as many seconds off the clock as she did. She made Colorado look like he'd been trained for barrel racing. *She's gutsy, that's all there is to it.*

Dylan peered through the entrance and saw Lani racing between the wall and the spread, with Colorado going great guns. As far as she could tell, there were no fences down. Dylan glanced at the clock. Fifty seconds! If Lani kept up this pace, she was going to finish at about one minute five. Lani landed clear of the spread and raced around the corner, looking over her shoulder at the next fences. Dylan worried that Colorado's stride was starting to look sloppy. *Tighten up*, she thought just as the pony seemed to slip. Dylan gasped as the pony struggled to keep his feet.

Lani sat back, letting Colorado regain his footing, but she slowed the pace considerably when she pointed him at the fence. Colorado was clearly shaken and tipped the top pole. Dylan held her breath. The pole bounced but stayed in place. Lani turned the pony for the final combination and asked him for more speed so he could clear the distance, but Colorado had lost his nerve. He swerved right around the jump.

Dylan's fingers tightened. *Come on, Colorado!* She was no longer thinking of her own place on the team but simply wanted her friend to finish the course. It had been such an amazing start! Lani took Colorado almost to the top of the ring before driving him strongly at the jump again. This time the gelding jumped. He was crooked, but he came through the in-and-out cleanly. Lani leaned forward and gave Colorado a generous pat before slowing him to a trot.

"Lani Hernandez on Colorado," the announcer said. "One minute, twenty-six seconds. Six time faults."

Applause filled the arena, acknowledging how well Lani had salvaged her round. But Dylan stood motionless, realizing she had made the team. The extra circle Lani had taken to redirect Colorado had cost her valuable time, and Dylan ended up with fewer faults.

"Get a move on, Walsh. You've got a ribbon with your name on it," Lani said, slipping her feet out of her stirrups. She was grinning broadly, genuinely pleased that one of them had made it.

Dylan didn't know what to say. Lani gave Colorado a good-bye pat as Sarah took his reins. "Have fun!" Lani said, rushing into the bleachers.

And then Malory shouted, her voice filled with excitement. "Dylan! Come on!"

Dylan ran over to Morello and, before putting her foot in the stirrup, she gave him a big hug. "You did it," she told him as she swung into the saddle, feeling as if her heart was going to explode with joy.

"Here." Malory steadied Hardy alongside Dylan and brushed a smudge of sawdust off her black coat. "We can't have you letting down the team. This is our grand entrance!"

"The team!" Dylan put her hands in the air, feeling triumphant, and Morello threw up his head at the sudden commotion.

"Trying out for cheerleading next?" Lynsey inquired as she rode past with Eleanor Dixon.

Dylan rolled her eyes behind Lynsey's back. "There's going to be no living with her now," she commented.

"Like there was before?" Malory smiled as they waited for Olivia Buckley to pass them, so they were all in order of how they had placed. Fourth up was Malory, who held her head high as she rode through the double doors to a storm of applause. Finally, Dylan followed. Coming fifth had earned her a place as the reserve rider for the team – and right now she couldn't be more thrilled if she'd come in first.

Ali Carmichael, Aiden Phillips, and Roger Musgrave were waiting for them in the centre of the arena, holding rosettes for the ponies and Chestnut Hill junior jumping team crests for the girls' riding jackets. The sound of cheers echoed around the arena. Dylan looked over and saw all the Adams girls sitting together. Lani let out a piercing whistle and stood up, clapping her hands over her head. "Way to go, Adams!" she shouted, and the rest of the Adams girls cheered even louder. Honey stood up and blew a congratulatory kiss.

Dylan had to steady Morello so that Ali Carmichael could pin the pink rosette on his bridle. "Great job, both of you," she said.

Dylan looked down at the crest her aunt was holding. The fabric badge displayed the same emblem as on the gates at the school entrance: a chestnut tree with leaf-laden branches and spreading roots and a horse's head.

"You did it the hard way, but you did it," Ali added, her eyes shining with warmth. "I'm really proud of you, Dylan."

The huge lump in Dylan's throat seemed to prevent her from finding the right words, so she just grinned.

At last the riding coaches stood back so that Eleanor Dixon could lead the team around the arena in a lap of honor.

Over the loudspeaker, Mr Musgrave announced, "Three cheers for this season's junior jumping team!"

As they cantered up the far side of the ring, Dylan had to hold Morello back. With each stride, he threatened to overtake Hardy. She knew exactly how the paint gelding was feeling. If it was up to her, she would be standing in her stirrups, racing ahead of them all, waving her crest in the air for everyone to see. Somehow, she managed to restrain herself and savour the moment.

Malory glanced back and met her eye, and Dylan could tell she was feeling just the same – and to think they had almost missed their chance.

When she came to the double doors, Eleanor Dixon led the other riders out onto the yard. It was still midday, and Dylan shielded her eyes as they adjusted to the sun. She didn't even realize that Lynsey had held back Bluegrass until he and Morello were walking side by side.

"Now that we're going to be spending even more time together, I thought you'd like to know something," Lynsey said, her eyes still focused on the path ahead.

Dylan frowned, distracted by the red rosette clipped to Bluegrass's bridle. "And what would that be?"

"I know you've somehow got it into your head that I was the one who called Ms Carmichael on you," Lynsey admitted, "but, as usual, you're completely off the mark."

"Just leave it, Lynsey," Dylan said, not wanting anything to spoil the afternoon. "It doesn't really matter now."

Lynsey shrugged. "Do you really think I would need to sabotage your getting on the team? I mean, Blue was a sure thing from day one. Think about it."

Before Lynsey had even finished, Bluegrass pulled ahead, and Dylan was left with her thoughts. *So what if it wasn't Lynsey?* she wondered. *Would someone else have wanted to keep me out of the tryouts? Did I really get it all wrong again?*

Why did Lynsey have to tell her this now? Dylan pulled Morello to a stop and dismounted, absentmindedly running up her stirrups. She clicked to Morello to walk forward, playing with his mane as her mind lingered on the possibilities.

"What do you think, boy?" she asked. Morello's eyes were half-closed and he gave a light snort. "I fully agree," Dylan responded with a smile. She convinced herself it really didn't matter – not today. Besides, she now had a much better sense of things, and she knew which girls she hoped would become her closest friends. She'd go with her gut and hope for the best.

Dylan was drawn from her thoughts by the sight of Lani and Honey tearing across the yard. "Dylan! Malory!" they yelled between gasps for breath.

Malory halted Hardy and waited with Dylan and Morello as Lani and Honey ran the rest of the way.

"You guys were brilliant!" Honey said, reaching up to give Morello a pat.

"They certainly were," Lani exclaimed, putting her hand on her chest with a dramatic flair. "You make us proud to be your roommates."

"Oh, Lani, you were so close to making it, too," Malory said with a hint of apology in her voice as they all headed toward the barn.

Lani shrugged. "You know, the better riders won, and all that."

Dylan wasn't sure she could have been as laid-back about not making the team, but she admired Lani's easygoing approach to everything.

"Besides," Lani added. "I don't think I could take any more of Lynsey Harrison than I absolutely have to."

Dylan and Malory exchanged knowing glances. Dylan noticed that Honey didn't say anything, and she assumed it was out of loyalty to their other roommate. And no one brought up Malory's near-departure. It felt like the distant past, and Dylan hoped it stayed that way. "Well, I have to admit, three Adams girls on the Chestnut Hill jumping team can't be bad," Dylan offered.

"And maybe even more next year," Malory added.

"That's right. We're taking over!" Lani announced.

"For now, how about we get the horses put away so we can go to the celebration buffet," Honey suggested.

"It's a plan," Lani said as she headed for the tack room with Hardy's saddle.

"I'm in," Malory confirmed before kissing Hardy on the forehead.

Dylan gave Morello a long pat. "Sounds perfect," she agreed. And, looking around at her new friends, Dylan realized that was just the right word. *Perfect*.

Look out for the next story in
Chestnut Hill

Chestnut Hill
Making Strides

an extract

Malory wanted to cheer along with everyone else after Dylan's solid finish, but it was her turn to jump. She scooped up the reins, trying not to think about the hundreds of eyes trained on her. *Please, please let me go clear*, she begged. It was her first official course after making the competition team, and she didn't want to let the other riders down. Even more, she wanted avoid being the target of Lynsey Harrison's petty taunts.

Hardy snatched at the reins as they cantered toward the red-and-white poles. "Steady," Malory whispered, holding her legs against him to maintain his bouncy stride but keeping a firm rein so that he wouldn't rush and flatten over the fence. Three yards away, she pushed her hands forward and let him take a fast, powerful stride before the jump. *Go, boy!* she thought as Hardy launched into the air.

The next two fences flashed past, and then they were cantering toward the parallel bars. Hardy listened to Malory right until he took off, forming a beautiful rounded arc over the fence. Malory felt a thrill of delight as she turned him to face the upright. *All of our practice has really paid off!* She relaxed a little as she judged the distance to their takeoff.

The next thing Malory knew, Hardy's nose was in the air and they were going too fast on the approach. When Hardy took the jump, he lost the graceful outline he had had over the previous fence. His forelegs knocked against the top pole, making it bounce in its holders. *Please stay up*, Malory prayed, not daring to look back and risk losing Hardy's focus again. The crowd groaned as the pole thudded onto the sand, and Malory felt her stomach drop with disappointment. She bit her lip and put a hundred and ten percent concentration into getting over the remaining jumps.

When Hardy landed clear over the final fence, the crowd burst into applause that was just as loud as for Dylan and Lynsey's rounds, but that didn't make Malory feel any better. She cantered back to the group, staring down at Hardy's mane. As far as she was concerned, she'd let the entire team down. It was not the ride the audience would have expected of the prestigious Rockwell Grant recipient.

"Good job," Eleanor mouthed.

Malory gave a half smile.

"That was great," Dylan whispered when Malory halted alongside her.

Malory watched Olivia fly around the course on - Shamrock. The dark grey mare pricked her ears as they raced toward the wall. "I feel like such an idiot for losing my concentration before the upright," she muttered.

"I think you're being too hard on yourself," Dylan replied. "I have no doubt that everyone in this arena thinks you did really well."

Malory couldn't help shooting a glance at Lynsey. As always, her round on Bluegrass had been flawless, and she would no doubt remind Malory of that fact.

Malory led Hardy into his stall, still feeling mad at herself for the dropped pole. Every other member of the team had gone clear. She listened to the running commentary Dylan was giving Morello in the next box stall. "You're going to get a treat tonight, boy. In fact, I might snag some apples from the dinner buffet. Or some carrot cake."

Malory rubbed Hardy's nose. *I hope Diane Rockwell wasn't here,* she thought, slipping the bridle over his ears. She didn't want to think that her scholarship might be in jeopardy if she didn't start turning in tight, clear rounds. Suddenly Hardy lifted his head and looked past her. The sound of lively, chatting voices came down the aisle and two tall young women looked over the door.

"You're Malory O'Neil, right?" said one of them. Her shining blond hair was cut into neat bangs that swept stylishly over her forehead, and her green eyes were bright and friendly as she smiled at Malory.

"That's me," Malory said, her brain whirring as she

tried to place the alumni, who somehow looked familiar.

"I'm Rachel and this is Sienna," the girl explained, placing a hand on the shoulder of her companion. *Lynsey's sisters!* With a jolt, Malory realized why they looked so familiar; they had the same sleek blond hair and high cheekbones, although Lynsey's eyes were a smoky blue, not green.

"We just wanted to congratulate you on your round," Rachel told her warmly. "You were great. I've never seen Hardy jump like that. He's been here since before I came to Chestnut Hill, and he was always so stubborn. But he looked like a champion out there, and I know he is a tricky pony to figure out."

Malory blinked. *Are you guys really related to Lynsey?* she wanted to ask. There was no way her classmate would have given her an ounce of credit for her riding today. "Thanks," she said, feeling her cheeks turn pink. "I just wish we'd gone clear! Hardy jumped his heart out, but I lost my concentration before that one fence."

"No worries," grinned Sienna. "It's still early in the year. I didn't ride here – I was on the tennis and field hockey teams – but even I can tell that it takes real talent to get this pony to look as good as he did. You two are quite the team. He'd jump mountains for you."

Malory was a little overwhelmed. It was clear that the sisters were going out of their way to be supportive of her. She was trying to think of a gracious reply when she saw Lynsey walking down the aisle.

"Well, I'll be around to see Lynsey at some of the shows," Rachel said. "I'll be on the lookout for you, Malory. I think you and Hardy could have quite a year."

Lynsey's eyes seemed to smolder, and all Malory could do was give Rachel and Sienna a tentative smile. She had a feeling that receiving compliments from the older Harrison sisters was not the best way to make nice with Lynsey.